PENGUIN BOOKS

# Entity

Meg Smitherman writes science fiction, fantasy and horror books (all of which involve kissing). She studied Creative Writing at Brunel University London, where she obtained both her MA and a staggering amount of student loan debt. When not writing, Meg spends her time playing video games, reading fan fiction and couch rotting. Based in Los Angeles, she shares her life with a chihuahua, a cat and a handsome Englishman.

CW01500830

# Entity

## MEG SMITHERMAN

PENGUIN BOOKS

PENGUIN BOOKS

UK | USA | Canada | Ireland | Australia
India | New Zealand | South Africa

Penguin Books is part of the Penguin Random House group of companies
whose addresses can be found at global.penguinrandomhouse.com

Penguin Random House UK,
One Embassy Gardens, 8 Viaduct Gardens, London SW11 7BW

penguin.co.uk

Penguin
Random House
UK

First self-published by Meg Smitherman 2025
First published in Great Britain by Penguin Books 2025

001

Set in 13.2/16pt Garamond MT
Typeset by Falcon Oast Graphic Art Ltd
Printed in Great Britain by Clays Ltd, Elcograf S.p.A.

The authorized representative in the EEA is Penguin Random House Ireland,
Morrison Chambers, 32 Nassau Street, Dublin D02 YH68

A CIP catalogue record for this book is available from the British Library

ISBN: 978-1-405-98702-8

Penguin Random House is committed to a sustainable future
for our business, our readers and our planet. This book is made from
Forest Stewardship Council® certified paper

The blackness of darkness supervened; all sensations appeared swallowed up in that mad rushing descent as of the soul into Hades. Then silence, and stillness, and night were the universe.

*The Pit and the Pendulum* by Edgar Allen Poe

# I

The lawyer slides a sheaf of papers across the wide leather seat. 'The NDA,' she says. 'Initial each page, and sign at the end.'

Unseasonal summer rain drums on the car roof. A fluorescent street light flickers in staccato as if it's Morse code, spelling out a message from the electric ether.

A steady drip from my trench is working hard to ruin the upholstery and soak into my skirt at the same time. In a deeply uncharacteristic move, I'd gone out into the downpour to wait for the car to pick me up fifteen minutes earlier than I needed to, convinced that if I was a second late, they'd change their minds. Usually, I'm late for everything.

'You did *read* the NDA?' the lawyer prompts, tapping the paper with a square burgundy nail. She studies me through a pair of wire-frame glasses, her gaze shrewd. I wonder if she disapproves of me, of this whole thing: the fact that some random twenty-something is being invited into the inner sanctum of our country's wealthiest and most reclusive man.

If I were Ian De Leon's lawyer, *I* would disapprove.

'Yeah,' I confirm, flipping through the contract.

Well . . . I've skimmed it. Mr De Leon's team advised me to have my lawyer look it over for my protection. Yeah, sure. My *lawyer*. Let me just hop in my private jet and go pick him up; we'll eat caviar and sip Dom Perignon while we peruse the NDA.

Understanding the contract won't make a difference to me anyway. I'm signing this thing no matter what. No freelance writer in her right mind would refuse an offer to write a book for Ian De Leon, no matter what the NDA says. This book is going to be a guaranteed bestseller, and that's an accolade I can ride for at least the next couple of years. Maybe even get an offer from a *real* publisher. One of the Big Two. And then? I'll be set. No more couch-surfing between one-night stands. No more bottle girl gigs; I don't give a *shit* how high they tip.

For a second, the reality of it all hits me, and I hesitate, fingers curling the corners of the NDA. Not for the first time, an insidious doubt nags at me. There's no way Ian De Leon *meant* to reach out to me with this job offer. He probably meant it for someone else. I write crackpot quantum physics theories on my blog, not biographies. I mean, I have a solid following, and occasionally, I get to write a paid article for some conspiracy theory site – worth it for the money, though a permanent knock to my ego – but how the hell did Ian even *hear* about me?

But there's no questioning where I am right now, the NDA in my hands. And there it is, my name typed right on the page, 'The Undersigned': Katherine Fox.

'You don't want to keep him waiting,' the lawyer prompts. Her hair is perfectly coiffed, a black bob that seems to defy gravity, sculpted into one solid wave.

'It's just . . .'

She raises her brows.

'This interview is for a book. It's going to be published. *Widely*. People will read it eventually.'

'Yes. But as you know, due to the highly sensitive nature of the product you'll be discussing, Mr De Leon has final say in what you include in the manuscript. If he wants to cut something, you will cut it. Our in-house publisher will also be under NDA. So, as agreed, since the manuscript will be approved by Mr De Leon and his legal team before publication, the contract stands. Nothing you see or discuss for the next three days will leave the premises without explicit permission from Mr De Leon.'

Fair enough.

I initial each page. I sign and date at the end.

'Thank you,' she says, gathering the contract and sliding it into a cream leather briefcase. 'I'll email you a copy for your records.'

'Thanks,' I say, buzzing with nerves like I've chugged three espressos in a row.

'Remember,' says the lawyer, 'from the moment

you leave this car, you're under NDA. No calls, texts, or photos. You'll be turning over your phone upon arrival. Mr De Leon will return it when you're finished.'

'What if there's an emergency?' I ask.

The lawyer looks at me in a way that says this was explicitly outlined in the contract, which I would have known had I read the fucking thing. She purses her lips. 'Mr De Leon has his own phone.'

'Okay.' The answer doesn't soothe me. I stare out the window, still dragging my feet for no reason. It's impossible to see anything through the rain-fogged glass but blurred flares of street lights and neon signs, and, above that, the looming dark monoliths of skyscrapers.

'Don't keep him waiting,' the lawyer says.

'Right.' I smile tightly and open the car door.

Rain pelts down from the gloomy evening sky. I grab my duffle and slide from the car, slamming the door behind me. I hurry across the pavement to the building doors, shivering in the cold wet. When I try to open them, I find they're locked. I glance over my shoulder, ready to ask the lawyer for help, but the car is already gone, the street empty and glistening with rain and reflections of light.

There's a buzzer by the door. I press it, and nothing happens. I see a reception desk inside, but nobody's there.

'Great,' I mutter. I take out my phone, flipping it open. Surely I'm allowed to call the lawyer. I hem and haw in the fluorescent glow of the building entrance.

Then something catches my eye, right at the periphery. A figure stands at the corner across the street, their silhouette illuminated by a street light.

A chill runs down my spine, and it has nothing to do with how cold I am. It's quiet for a Friday evening in downtown LA. This place should be crawling with traffic. Craning my neck, I look up at the towering building. It's so tall it may as well be jutting into space, its apex obscured by rainfall. Purple lights brighten its edges, but it's otherwise dark; there are no yellow-lit windows to indicate anyone's there. For all I know, this building is completely empty except for the penthouse, where Ian De Leon lives.

And then it occurs to me that this building looks familiar. I remember it being built not too long ago. A few years, maybe. So many mega skyscrapers have sprung up all over LA that I can't keep track. It's like an entire skyline of Burj Khalifas. But something about this particular building pulls at my curiosity, drawing me in.

I press the buzzer again. A sudden lance of fear cuts through me: Am I in the right place? Is this an elaborate scam? There's been a spate of disappearances lately in downtown LA – am I about to be the next? What if I just willingly human trafficked myself?

Heart in my throat, I turn, looking for I don't know what – a street sign, the lawyer's car, something to anchor me.

The figure across the street is still there, a tall black silhouette. My breath catches. But as I watch, the figure seems to flicker, dissipating in the rain.

What the fuck? Did I imagine it?

A sound distracts me, pulling my attention back to the building. A square-shaped panel has opened above the buzzer, revealing a clear black plane of glass. I slap my palm on the glass for a fingerprint read, and a red light scans across my splayed hand.

The buzzer emits a loud, abrasive beep, making me jump.

Then nothing.

I glance over my shoulder. The figure is gone. A chill grips my chest, and I place my hand on the black glass again. The red light scans me, beeps loudly, and doesn't do anything.

'Let me the fuck *in*,' I mutter, unable to stop the fight or flight response my body is deciding I need right now. Then I realize it might not be a hand scanner.

I lean forward and line up my eye with the black glass. The red light almost blinds me as it scans across my vision.

The glass flashes.

*Bzzzt!* The door unlocks.

Tingling with adrenaline, I hurry through the door and let it slam shut behind me, the lock clicking decisively into place. I turn to look back into the street, searching for that figure again.

The street is empty, wet, reflecting an impression-istic painting of the cityscape.

'Jesus,' I murmur under my breath. 'I need to stop watching horror movies before bed.'

I see an elevator bank to the right and head toward it, choosing not to view the disappearing figure as a bad omen. All that woo-woo shit can be bad for you in high doses; I choose to keep mine confined to my blog. At the elevators, I press the up button and become painfully aware of my bare, chewed-up nails. I should have had them done before I came. The lawyer's nails were pristine, shiny, and rich. Ian De Leon is going to take one look at me and throw me out.

'You can't even afford *rent*, Kit,' I say aloud, chiding. 'Let alone a manicure. That's why you're here.'

But if I'm being honest with myself, I would have taken the gig for free. Anyone would. My writing career is about to take off in a way I could never have done on my own. In reality, I should have had to fight off thousands of award-winning writers and journalists just for a chance to write this book for Ian De Leon. But he came to *me*. He wanted *me*.

*Ding!*

One of the elevators opens.

I step inside, pressing the button for the penthouse.

My trench drips steadily on the floor as I ascend 153 floors.

It's utterly quiet in the elevator but for the low hum

7

of upward movement. I'm trying to wring the water out of my coat when an uncanny sensation comes over me. For a second, I feel like I'm having a déjà vu. Like I've been here before, in this very elevator, my pale fingers twisting the dark green fabric of my second-hand trench. But not just that — I feel like I'm going underwater, like I'm falling, sinking deep, my eyes and ears filling up. And for a split second, I almost think . . .

I almost think the whole world flickers out of view. As if every light in the universe had gone dark, and —

My ears pop painfully.

The sensation is gone.

And the elevator comes to a smooth, almost imperceptible stop. There's a soft chime, and the doors slide open.

I hesitate for a breath, disoriented. I'm not used to riding in such fast elevators. The altitude change really did a number on me. But I'm *here*. And that excitement, the reality of it, washes away my anxiety.

I step out of the elevator onto plush carpet and immediately freeze. Glancing around at the living space, the first word that occurs to me is *pristine*. I've never seen a living area so large and so visibly untouched. It's open plan, all chrome and dark wood and strangely shaped cream sofas that almost look like art installations. On the far wall, facing west, is a single floor-to-ceiling window through which the facades of nearby skyscrapers, glittering with animated ads, glow neon in rain-blurred smears.

God, everything in this place is so *clean*. I'm going to ruin Ian De Leon's penthouse with rainwater and street grime. Here come my nerves, back again to play. But I refuse to let them. I'm supposed to be here. I signed a contract.

No one is here to greet me, though, except a seemingly empty penthouse.

'Hello?' I say, bending down to unlace my boots. There's no way I'm tracking water and dirt all over a billionaire's house.

'Yeah, come in,' comes a voice from around the corner of the elevator bay.

Anticipation licks my skin. I know that voice. It's one of the most famous voices in the world, and also one of the wealthiest.

Awkwardly, I shake my boots off. Should I just leave them by the door? What about my duffle?

'Mr De Leon,' I say, 'where can I put my wet things?'

'There's a closet to the left, in the hallway. Come in, come in.'

'Okay, thanks,' I reply, feeling incredibly awkward. Shouldn't he have a butler? And where is his Eros model, if not here to greet me? Maybe he's saving the reveal for later.

I find the closet, but not without leaving a dripping path in my wake. The closet is empty except for a line of slippers in various sizes on the floor. I hang up my damp coat, delicately place my boots and duffle in the far corner, and then stare hesitantly at the slippers. Should I put some on? Is that what they're for?

After a moment of waffling, I finally slide my feet into one of the smallest pairs. Then I remember I'm supposed to turn in my phone and pluck it from my handbag before hanging that up, too. I close the closet door.

My heart is hammering. Now that I'm out of the rain with dry feet, it's starting to really hit me: I'm alone in a sky-high penthouse with Ian De Leon.

*Ian De Leon!*

'Found it?' my host calls, probably wondering why I'm taking so long.

'Yeah, sorry!' I follow his voice to the other side of the elevator, where a kitchen and bar open up in warmly lit hues. And there, standing behind the bar with a bottle of whiskey in his hand, is Ian De Leon.

He smiles, and I already know he's going to be a problem for me. 'What are you drinking, Katherine Fox?'

## 2

Ian De Leon is shorter than I thought he'd be. I've only seen him in photographs from before he made all his money, or in the official-looking headshots they use in the news. Not a single paparazzi shot of him exists, and he doesn't do interviews. Not since the Eros model debuted. In fact, for years he's said he would never appear in public or give an interview again.

Until now.

He's older than his most recent photo by about a decade, putting him . . . mid-forties, I'm guessing. His thick black hair is marked at the temples with streaks of silver. His jaw is stubbled with five-o'clock shadow, which I suspect is by design. His collared white shirt hangs open at the throat, revealing a thin gold chain and a hint of chest hair. A pair of round, gold-framed glasses hang from his shirt pocket. Everything about him is perfect, clean, curated – just like the penthouse.

Ian De Leon is *much* better looking in person. And even though I try to ignore it, my heart rate absolutely can't. He is definitely going to be a problem.

Rain patters the floor-to-ceiling window behind me.

Ian watches me expectantly with dark brown eyes. And as I move closer, pulse pounding, something in his gaze makes my gut tighten. He looks like the men I used to serve at cocktail bars: polite at first, even respectful, but deep down I recognize a glint of hunger there.

He clears his throat.

I realize he's waiting for my answer. I try to relax; I need to chill the fuck out if I'm going to spend the next three days with him. 'Whiskey's fine.'

He raises a dark eyebrow. 'Straight?'

'Oh . . . uh, no.' I'm so off my game. Usually, I'm a pro at acting cool and casual, no matter what emotions are scrabbling for purchase underneath. 'Sorry, I thought . . . because you had the bottle –'

He leans over the bar, forearms resting on the countertop. His sleeves are rolled up to the elbow, revealing a gold bracelet partially obscured by thick dark hair. 'Tell me what you'd order from the bar,' he says with a half-smile. His mannerisms are disarming, intimate, and a little too sexy.

I almost blurt out my actual order – a shot of tequila – like I'm sixteen with a fake ID. But Ian De Leon doesn't need to know how cheap a date I really am, how easy it is to get me into . . . *well*. In any other circumstance, I'd fall into his bed stone-cold sober. But in this case, I'm trying to be a professional career woman; a person who drinks fancy cocktails. And I'm ashamed to realize I have no idea what drink I should want. What cocktails do women in their twenties with generational wealth order at the bar?

I go with the safest route. 'I'll have what you're having.'

He smiles. 'One Sazerac, coming right up.'

Whatever that is. 'Perfect.'

He rummages around the bar, pulling out ingredients. 'Katherine. Is that your preferred name?'

His voice curls around my name like thick smoke. I lick my lips. 'Kit. If you'd rather use a nickname, my friends call me Kit.'

He returns to the bar with another bottle of liquor – something green – and a few other things. 'Kit,' he says thoughtfully, pouring the green liquid into a glass and swirling it. 'Call me Ian.'

'Okay. Ian.'

'I'm excited to have you here, Kit,' he says, muddling sugar and what I think is bitters in another glass. 'I have so much to show you. We have so much to talk about.'

No fucking kidding. I bite my lip to hold back what I really want to say, which is an uninterrupted string of words and questions about the Eros model, what it means, how it could change our culture as a whole, the philosophical implications, the *religious* implications . . . but we have three whole days for that. And I'm determined to play it cool, even though I've failed at it so far. I don't want him to think I'm a stalker, never mind that *he* invited *me* here.

'Yeah, I'm excited, too,' I say. Understatement of the millennium. And then, because I just can't help myself, 'What you're doing with the robotics field is honestly mind-blowing. No one's ever –'

He holds up a finger, shaking his head. 'Please, no flattery. You're not here as a sycophant. I've got plenty of those. Plenty. We're intellectuals, Kit. You and I. The world may not see it that way, but you have *ideas*. That blog of yours – ah, that reminds me.' He snaps a finger, holding out his hand, palm up. 'Phone, please.'

'Oh, right, sorry.' I've been holding it in my sweaty hand this whole time. I wipe the phone surreptitiously on my skirt, and hand it over, his words circling giddily in my head: *We're intellectuals. You and I.*

He grins, white teeth flashing, and drops the phone into his pants pocket. 'Now, we're free,' he says. 'Nothing to distract, nothing to interfere.'

I'm not sure how to answer, so I just smile back.

I'm relieved when he finally finishes making our drinks and holds one out to me. I need to loosen up before he changes his mind about this whole thing and sends me packing.

'Tell me what you think,' Ian says, before sipping his own. He closes his eyes, adopting an expression of utter bliss. 'Wow,' he murmurs. 'Wow! Nothing better. Nothing better.'

I sip mine, hyper-aware of how heavy the glass is, how it must be crystal. The liquid slides easily down my throat, and I relish the warm burn. It has a strange licorice aftertaste, but it goes down smooth. 'I like it, thank you.'

'Good,' he says. 'Are you hungry?'

'I'm actually starving,' I admit. I've been too anxious to eat all day. But now that I'm here, sipping a Sazerac, the nerves are wearing off, and my appetite has come roaring back.

Ian grins. 'You like steak?'

'Of course.'

He points at me. 'Let me guess. Medium?'

'Rare, actually.'

He laughs. 'Girl after my own heart. Two rare steaks, coming right up. We'll talk while I cook.'

I follow Ian into the adjacent kitchen. I try to drink slowly, but every sip relaxes me. And I need to relax. I take a seat at a generous kitchen island with a black granite countertop and watch as Ian moves competently about the kitchen, pulling out ingredients.

'Do you cook often?' I ask.

'Hardly ever,' he says. 'You like potatoes? Or salad?'

'I like both.'

He claps his hands together once. 'Both! Good girl. So. The book. What's your vision?'

'Oh,' I say, caught off guard. 'I thought – I mean, I'm meant to be your ghostwriter, right? The vision should be yours. Do you need help with dinner?'

Ian, midway through chopping a head of garlic,

pauses to shoot me a look over his shoulder. 'I'm all good. I'm very particular about my food. And you're not a ghostwriter. You'll get full author credit. It's a biography, not an autobiography. You read the contract, right?'

'Yeah, yeah,' I say hurriedly, the words sinking in. *Full author credit.* 'Sorry, I'm just . . .'

'Drink up,' Ian says. 'You're nervous. I get it. Weird building, weird guy living in it, weird everything. I get it. But we're friends now. Is that okay with you? We're not coworkers; I'm not your boss. We're friends. So, tell me. What's the vision?'

I take another long sip of my drink. The liquid warms me from my throat all the way down to my stomach. 'To be honest, I hadn't thought about it that much. I mean, I *have*, but I was hoping to meet the Eros model and learn more about it first. And more about you. The standard would be, you know, early life, and then your career, and then –'

Ian turns to face me, waving a knife with dissatisfaction. 'No, no. Early life? Boring. I want to get right into it. The book starts with Eros. *He's* the one who matters. Everything before him is irrelevant. Totally irrelevant.'

I sip my drink. 'Makes total sense.' Why did he ask me for my vision if he has one already? The smell of garlic and onion fills my nostrils, and the alcohol is finally loosening me up.

'The thing is, Kit, no one's doing what I am. Not

in artificial intelligence, not in robotics, not in the sex industry. I'm leagues above every other entrepreneur in the country, probably the world. Right? But that's . . . that's not the book. You're the book. Your take on everything, on me, on Eros. Your mind is something else. You're like me. You see things no one else does. You want mashed or boiled?'

I stare. 'I . . . what?'

'Potatoes.'

'Oh! Whatever you want is fine.'

He returns my stare. 'Mashed or boiled? Either way, they'll be drowning in garlic butter and herbs.'

'Boiled.'

'Boiled it is.' He claps once, digs around in a cupboard, and pulls out a bag of new potatoes.

By the time dinner is ready, I've finished my drink. I'm pleasantly buzzed, the alcohol working wonders on my empty stomach. Ian lays out our food on the kitchen island, pulling up a stool next to me.

'Dig in,' he says, then follows his own instruction.

As we eat, Ian makes no attempt at conversation. He's single-minded, maybe even distracted. I get the impression he doesn't host much, if at all. The second he finishes eating, he hops off his stool and goes straight to the bar. Still working on my steak, I can't help but watch him as he goes, his broad shoulders, the way his dark grey slacks hug his figure. And I notice for the first time that he's barefoot.

'Another?' he calls back to me, holding up the whiskey.

I nod. 'Yes, please.'

I finish my steak as he prepares our drinks, and I slide awkwardly off the stool. I begin stacking up our dishes to wash up, but Ian clicks his tongue, stopping me.

'No, no,' he says. 'Don't bother, I'll do it. Later. Come on. Let's sit.' He holds out a second drink.

'Thanks for dinner,' I say, taking the drink and letting Ian lead us into the living area.

'You're welcome,' he says, flopping onto one of the architectural sofas. 'Sit.' He holds out a hand to indicate the spot next to him. He settles in, folding one leg under the other.

I hesitate.

The rain outside is relentless, streaking the massive window in wavering luminous color. Beyond, the cityscape is ephemeral and coldly dark. But in here, the lights are warm. It smells of garlic and onion, and faintly of something musky – probably Ian's cologne.

'I won't bite,' he says. 'Come on, Kit. We're friends. Sit, sit.'

'My skirt is still a little damp,' I protest weakly. 'Your sofa –'

'I don't give a shit,' he says impatiently. He sips his drink, a gold signet pinky ring glinting in the lamplight. 'Sit, please.'

I finally relent, perching at the edge of the sofa like a bird ready to take flight.

'So,' says Ian, the sharpness gone from his voice. He's even more attractive here, lit softly at the edges, only the palest hues of purple and red playing on his skin from neon ads outside. His dark features are rugged but statuesque, refined but dangerous. 'Your blog. What's the deal there? No one else likes it? Why haven't I seen you in *Scientific American* or something?'

I blink, shocked briefly into silence.

'Well?'

'Um, the deal is I'm not a scientist,' I answer, feeling both flattered and incredibly embarrassed. 'I'm sure you've seen that none of my pieces are peer-reviewed. I mean, I love what I write, I believe in it, but it's frankly kind of insane. Like . . . science fiction shit.'

'Fuck that,' Ian says, waving a hand. 'Peer-reviewed my ass. That's the establishment. Society wants to keep us in a cage, Kit. My ideas were science fiction once, too. Do you see me in a goddamn cage?'

A little thrill rolls through me. 'No.'

'Because I didn't let them convince me I was crazy. Because I'm not. I'm a fucking genius. And so are you, okay? I've read your whole blog. It's groundbreaking. Really cool shit. And I want you to put it in the book. Incorporate it. Eros, consciousness, multiverse theory, wormholes, lizardmen, whatever. All of it.'

'I never wrote about lizard –'

'I'm trying to make a point, Kit. This book won't just change your life. It'll make you famous. It'll make you rich. And it'll also change the world. All you need is a legitimate platform. I'm your platform.'

I down half my drink, skin tingling with anticipation and a sense of unreality. Ian De Leon read my entire blog. He took it seriously. He takes *me* seriously. I knew there was a reason he reached out to me to write his book. I knew it logically, but . . . it hadn't quite hit home until now.

The realization alone is enough to make me feel drunk. Or maybe it's the two Sazeracs doing their work. I inch closer to Ian, holding his gaze. 'When do I get to see the Eros model?' The question comes out before I have a chance to stop myself. I had been trying to be patient, to not act like some kind of weird groupie. But Ian sees me as an intellectual equal, and I'm hungry to see Ian's incredible invention.

'Call him Eros,' Ian says. 'Not a *model*. That makes him sound like a product.'

'He is.'

'He's more than that.' Ian holds my gaze with his sharp one. 'You know that. Don't fuck with me.'

'I'm not —'

He leans toward me almost intimately, and my words fall away. 'I want you to write this book because you're special,' Ian says. 'Your ideas are special. But you can't meet Eros tonight.'

I'm disappointed, but not as much as I should be. I'm finding myself increasingly distracted by Ian's closeness, the smell of him, how unexpectedly hot he is. 'Why not?'

The corner of Ian's mouth quirks. 'I want you sober when you meet him. Tonight's for fun. You want another drink?'

I can't imagine why I need to be sober when I meet Eros. Probably so I can fully appreciate the engineering miracle that he is, though I'm sure I'd appreciate that at any state of inebriation. 'Yes, please.'

Ian smiles. 'Coming right up.'

# 3

By the time we're finishing our third round, Ian has covered all the small talk basics. Veering suddenly away from the book and Eros, he started asking about *me*. Where I'm from, what I studied, if I have any pets, my parents' names, and – he wheedled it out of me – my actual bar order.

I'm no longer nervous or stilted. This feels like a night in with a friend. Ian is weird, but charming when he wants to be, and I don't mind looking at him. I don't mind the way his eyes follow my movements, the way his gaze lingers on my mouth. And I feel *interesting*, for the first time in a long time. Maybe for the first time in my life. I feel seen by Ian. Understood in a way I've never been understood. He's asking me questions my ex didn't think to ask until we'd been dating for months. And on top of all that, he even loves my blog.

And the excitement of tomorrow, the knowledge that I'll be meeting Eros, *speaking* to him, buzzes in my skull like a heady drug.

'Tequila shot?' Ian asks, rising from the couch, half-smiling. I can't tell if he's joking. He's just as perfectly groomed as he was before we started drinking with only a hint of dishevelment: one dark curl falling loose over his forehead.

If I'm being honest with myself, I want another. I want to sink into the softly-lit haze of drunkenness. I want to immerse myself in this indulgence, this validation I've been waiting my whole life to receive. But I'm also well aware that I'm here for work, and another drink will send me right over the edge. 'I'm okay, thanks though.'

Ian smiles conspiratorially. 'I won't tell anyone.'

'We should get an early start tomorrow.'

'We'll be fine.' He holds out his hand for my glass.

A self-loathing laugh threatens to bubble up my throat. I know what's going to happen next. I know who I am. I know what I'm like.

'C'mon,' Ian urges. 'C'mon.' He smiles wide, and I can't help the way my skin tingles at the sight. He's magnificently hot.

Fuck it. I hand over my glass.

While Ian is at the bar, I stand and go to the floor-to-ceiling window. I drift closer to the glass. I've never been this high up before. Rain still pounds the glass, but I bet you could see the ocean from here on a clear day. I wonder if Ian ever stands here and gazes out over the west side of the city, searching for inspiration.

'Afraid of heights?' Ian asks.

'Not really.' I stop a few inches from the glass.

Police drones buzz through the night, their red lights flashing below me, spotlights beaming down through a thick fog onto the streets below. I can see everything from up here. The city is dark but vivid, all its light and color bleeding together against towering buildings, and . . . oh, *fuck*.

I sway, pressing a palm to the glass. Either I'm way more intoxicated than I thought, which isn't likely, or I've developed sudden altophobia. My vision spins, then pops and crackles like an antique TV screen. The cityscape flickers in and out. Towers of light disappear and reappear again under a stormy sky.

How many shots were in those cocktails?

Sick with vertigo, not trusting myself to stay upright, I close my eyes and lean my forehead against the glass.

That was the wrong thing to do.

As soon as I close my eyes, I get a sickening swooping feeling in my gut, like I'm falling through the glass and into the rainy night, plummeting downward into a black abyss. It's the same sensation I felt in the elevator, like I'm deep underwater, but more intense. The world is opening up before me, and there's an impossible pressure crushing me, grinding my bones, flattening my lungs.

But something tells me it won't last forever. If I can just hold out, if I can get to the other side –

'Kit.' Ian's voice is sharp.

I gasp, opening my eyes. The city spreads out before me, rain-blurred and bright.

I step back from the glass, unsteady on my feet.

'You good?' I turn to see Ian standing by the couch, watching me. His expression is unreadable. He's holding a full shot glass in one hand, a bottle of water in the other. He smiles slowly. 'I thought you weren't afraid of heights.'

I return to the couch, taking the offered drinks. His eyes flit to my shaking fingers, and I'm ashamed. I wait for him to scold me, to say something like he refuses to work with someone who can't handle her liquor, who can't handle being 153 stories in the air. Instead, he waits patiently for me to settle in, to take a revitalizing sip of water. He watches me take the shot, his gaze piercing.

When I'm warm from tequila, my heart finally begins to slow, and I meet his penetrating stare. 'Sorry about that,' I murmur. 'I've never actually been in a building this tall.'

He takes the shot glass from me, his fingers brushing mine. There are a few drops left. He dips his finger into the glass, collecting the last of the tequila, and deposits it on his tongue. He swallows. 'I should have warned you. It's a ridiculous building, gives everyone vertigo. Too tall. Way too tall.' He laughs like it's hilarious that he owns a penthouse in a building that's practically in space. 'Takes some getting used to.'

I can't help but smile back at him. 'The tequila helped.'

He sets the shot glass on a side table, then props an elbow on the back of the couch, leaning in toward me. 'Let me distract you, Kit. Is that okay?'

I don't know what he means by *distract*, but I want it, whatever it is. I nod.

'Tell me something,' he says, voice low, taking advantage of our close proximity. 'Do you know why I do what I do?'

The tequila has me loose, relaxed, and warm. Rain patters the window in a soothing rhythm. Ian's gaze is soft. I set my water next to the shot glass, allowing my body to lean toward Ian's. I know what he's doing. I've played this game a thousand times, and I'm good at it. 'I don't know, Ian. Why do you do what you do?'

His eyes crinkle at the corners when I say his name. 'Because we are more than our basest functions. We are intellect. Emotion. Curiosity. These things make us what we are. But if you take away those higher functions, then what?'

'We're no more than animals,' I answer, a thrill running through me. This is the kind of thing I love to write about on my blog. 'Or worse, we're vegetative. Walking the line between life and death.'

'Exactly,' Ian says proudly, like I'm his prize pupil. 'But what if we take away the lower, base, simplest functions of a human? You take away fear, hunger,

27

the need to reproduce . . . you take away *death*. What do we have then?'

I know what he would answer. *Without his base urges, a human becomes nothing more than a computer*. It's one of his most famous quotes. But I don't want to repeat his words back to him like a fangirl. I want to prove that I'm worthy of his respect. 'A higher being,' I answer. 'A sentience no longer weighed down by its physical needs. Maybe even the next evolution of humanity.'

His smile broadens. 'I love the way you think.'

'Thank you,' I say, and I feel a telltale blush rising on my cheeks. Fucking embarrassing.

'I'm not flattering you. I'm being honest.' Ian is very much in my personal space, one arm braced against the back of the couch, one gesturing as he talks. Our knees are almost touching. 'I'm curious. Do you believe this so-called *higher being*, this next evolution of human-ity . . . can it possess both, and still remain superior? The intellect . . .' he leans closer, and suddenly his thumb is on my chin, his eyes searching mine. 'And the base urges?'

The room is very warm, its edges liquor-hazy. The rain is picking up, and the wind howls outside, ani-malistic. But Ian's thumb on my chin insists that I stay focused on him, on the question. The room fades away, and nothing is left but Ian's dark eyes, his jaw, the curl of hair on his forehead.

'What if the urges were controlled by outside, or

artificial means?' he continues. 'What if they were limited, unable to override the higher functions? Can such a thing claim to be superior? Or is it only a mockery, a facsimile, of what already exists?'

My lips part. Ian's gaze flickers down to my mouth. My brain stalls out. Then I realize he's waiting for me to respond. 'If you were able to isolate the lower functions,' I say, 'to control them as you say, so they never overwhelm the mind . . . then whatever you've created is no longer human. Humans lose control all the time. We think we're governed by our intellect, but we're not. We're barely a step above an animal.'

'We roll in the mud with the beasts,' he says.

'I guess we do.'

Then he leans forward, thumb still on my chin, and kisses me.

It's wildly unprofessional.

It's hot as fuck.

I know I should push him away and put a stop to this. It can't go anywhere; it creates a weird dynamic, he's twice my age – I even saw it coming and didn't stop it. But I still want it.

I've been wanting to kiss Ian De Leon since I first saw him.

He tastes like whiskey. He kisses like he's spent years perfecting the art. If he'd slobbered on me, if he'd been desperate and pawed at me, I could have easily cut this short. But he hasn't. And he doesn't. He stays exactly where he is, his fingers holding my chin, our knees almost touching.

And even though we're just kissing, I'm slowly undone. I was already horny for him, but now? I'm four drinks in, and I can barely restrain myself from crawling into Ian's lap and ripping his shirt open. It's what I'd normally do in this situation.

But I do have some self-control. *Some.*

When he makes a soft, low sound in his throat, I almost change my mind and straddle him. But a distant, insistent thought keeps hounding me: this is *work*. I'm at *work*. This is my boss, no matter what he says about us being 'friends'. And I'm acting like my usual fuck-up self.

Ian's thumb runs slowly along my jaw. It's the only place he's touching me, but the sensation is like a live wire to my skin. I lean into the feeling, hating myself for doing so. Hating that when he deepens the kiss, tilting his head to let my tongue in, I eagerly take the invitation. Hating the way my body betrays me, the breathiness, the involuntary moans.

By the time Ian pulls away to end the kiss, I'm wet and thoroughly disgusted with myself.

'Good, Kit,' Ian says, his thumb returning softly to my chin. His pupils are dark. My traitor eyes flit down, and I see that he's just as turned on as I am. 'Good.'

'I probably shouldn't have let you do that,' I murmur. A massive understatement.

'Why not?' he asks, leaning back, giving me a little space. 'You've been checking me out all night. If you weren't so focused on making a good impression, you would have noticed I was checking you out, too. That little skirt is incredibly fucking sexy.' He lets his gaze rake over me slowly. I revel in it. 'Are we wrong for feeling these things?' he continues. 'Are we not allowed to act on them?'

I take a steadying breath. It's not like I've never made out with an authority figure before. And I'll only be here for three days. What could possibly go wrong in that time? 'Just promise you won't fire me for kissing you.'

'I kissed *you*, Kit.'

'You know what I mean.'

'I told you, I'm not your boss. We're friends. I wasn't fucking with you. We're getting to know each other. I'm getting to know you. Am I supposed to let just anyone write this book for me?'

'Right,' I say. 'No, totally.'

He stands, looming over me, impossibly sexy. His shirt hangs open, his thick black hair now slightly more mussed from the kiss. Was I grabbing his hair? I don't remember. I must have been. My slut hands.

He smiles, and his gaze is on fire. 'Get your bag. I'll take you to your room.'

As I stand and retrieve my duffle from the closet, following him up a black spiral staircase, I allow the worst version of myself to come out. I wonder what he'd do if I tried to take him to bed. Would he refuse? Of course he wouldn't. Men never do. And he's still hard. He'd be such an easy lay, and I can see that he has plenty to work with. We've already kissed. Would fucking be so much worse?

I'm gnawing at my lip with anticipation as Ian leads me to a large, clean guest room. A window looks out onto the night, the steady rain. He turns on the lights, ushering me in. 'Your home for the next few days.'

I turn to face him. He's leaning against the door frame, hair hanging over his forehead, chest hair on full display, erection also on full display. My mouth waters. I say nothing.

'Good night, Kit.'

I have about two seconds to decide what kind of idiot to be.

He straightens and starts to turn.

'Ian,' I blurt.

He pauses and turns to face me, brows raised. There's a spark of something like approval behind his eyes. Like maybe he wants this, too.

'Do you want to . . .' I bite my lip, tilting my head to indicate the room behind me, the bed.

He hesitates, and my heart stands still. I can't tell what he's thinking, but he studies me for a moment, allowing his gaze to travel up from my feet to my breasts to my face, where he lingers.

*God*, I want him. Say yes, say yes, please . . .

After a long silence in which I almost spontaneously combust, Ian speaks. 'Good night, Kit.'

Then he turns and closes the door behind him.

And I'm left standing there alone, burning up with arousal and shame.

# 4

I wake up soon after sunrise. The remains of a dream fade from my mind like wisps of smoke, and as I blink awake, I try to grasp at them, pulling them to me for comfort. It was a sweet dream, familiar, like sinking into a warm bath. But I can't remember the details. All I recall is a *feeling*, and arms around me, and knowing I was safe.

Rolling over onto my stomach, I groan into the pillow as the waking world takes hold. And then I remember last night.

I take a moment to wallow in embarrassment, staring out at the fog-thick city. It's still raining. My head hurts, but it's nothing a little water won't fix.

Groaning, I roll out of bed and rummage in my duffle. I haven't properly unpacked, and my duffle and the surrounding floor already look like an explosion site. Locating a comfortable pair of jeans and my favorite sweater, I dress quickly, shoving my recording device into my back pocket.

As I brush my teeth in the en suite, I stare at myself in the mirror, eyeing my dyed blonde hair and its dark roots. I stand out like a trashy thumb in these expensive surroundings. I wish I could undo all the mistakes from last night. The booze, the kiss, the pathetic invitation to bed. But if I'm already wishing, I may as well wish to undo all the other nights just like it.

Sighing, I pull my hair into a loose braid. Then I wash my face, swipe on some mascara, and call it good enough. If I make too much of an effort, Ian will think I'm trying to seduce him. He *already* thinks that.

'God, Katherine,' I say aloud to my reflection. My eyes are red-rimmed, my pale skin flushed with emotion. 'You really can't help yourself, can you?'

Unable to stand the sight of myself any longer, I turn back to the bedroom, staring listlessly out the window. The clouds are so low they're almost on top of us, neon advertisements lighting up their undersides. I go to the window, determined to overcome the fear I felt last night. Maybe I can make myself into someone useful, piece by piece, if I try very hard.

I press my palm to the glass. It's cold, foggy with condensation, and I imagine I can almost feel the rain on the other side, wind-lashed and icy.

Something buzzes through me all at once: excitement? Terror? Arousal? I gasp, closing my eyes, and suddenly I'm falling again. Tumbling out into the morning, the skyline needle-like below me. And then the abyss rises up, swallowing the skyline. Black. Endless. The abyss is a crack in the sky, or in my chest, and I'm drawn into it, slowly crushed under the pressure, unable to –

There's a sharp knock at my door.

I jerk back to the moment, breathing hard.

'Just a second!' I call out, sitting on the edge of the bed. I take a few deep breaths, waiting for my adrenaline to chill. It's the height. It's fine. I'll just stop looking out the windows.

When my heartbeat finally starts to slow, I go to the door and open it.

Ian stands outside, holding a steaming mug. He looks just as appealing this morning as he did last night, I notice with a pang of annoyance. 'I thought you might need help with your early start.'

'Thanks,' I say, taking the mug. He seems . . . normal. Not avoiding my gaze, and he's obviously not planning on kicking me out. Maybe my drunken antics really weren't that bad. By the time we get downstairs, my spirits are a little higher.

I also can't help but notice that Ian is dressed just as impeccably as last night, in black slacks and a grey Henley that looks like cashmere. But unlike last night, the round glasses are perched on Ian's nose.

I swallow dryly, then take a much-needed sip of coffee. I was such an idiot to let him kiss me. Now that I know how good he tastes, I'll never stop wanting him.

'Are you hungry?' he asks, gesturing toward the kitchen. 'I have eggs, bacon, toast. I don't cook much, but when I do, breakfast is my specialty.'

My stomach turns, a memory of too much to drink.

I wrap both hands around my mug. 'I'm okay for now. Just coffee's good.'

He nods, smiling. 'Sleep well? Ready to get started? Ready to meet Eros?'

'Yes,' I blurt, skin tingling with anticipation. Just the mention of Eros revives me, energizes me. 'Of course, yes to all of it. May I start recording?'

Ian steers me away from the kitchen, toward a nondescript door in the far wall. 'You may.'

Reaching into my back pocket, I pull out my recorder and press the red circle. The light flashes on, and I check to make sure I have enough battery life. Everything looks good.

'I have a question to start us off,' I say, sliding the device back into my pocket.

Ian unlocks the door by typing in a code on a small panel. Cool air rushes out to greet us when the door swings open. He ushers me inside a dark space, one hand at the small of my back. My skin alights at the touch. What is his *deal*? Is he teasing me?

Then lights flicker on, illuminating a descending stairwell.

'Ask away,' Ian says.

'Why did you get me drunk last night?' I can't help myself. I want to know for the sake of my pride. 'It wasn't to seduce me.'

'Did I get you drunk?' Ian says, beginning to descend. He gestures for me to follow, so I do.

'Three cocktails and a shot of tequila?' I prompt.

My slippers pad softly on hard metal stairs. Ian is still, bizarrely, barefoot. He says nothing.

'You offered me a drink the second I got here,' I push on. 'And when I let you choose my poison, you served me what amounts to straight whiskey with a dash of sugar and absinthe. And you kissed me.'

He stops on the stairs. I stop two stairs behind him, and when he turns to face me, we're almost eye to eye. His gaze is mild, amused.

'You *weren't* trying to get me drunk, Ian?'

He looks me up and down, smiling softly. 'You were nervous when you got here. You were sexy. And I got the impression you liked the kiss.'

I grit my teeth, pushing past him to continue down the stairs. 'You put me in a position to humiliate myself.'

He follows close behind. 'Humiliate? Where? I don't see humiliation. I see a woman who knows what she wants. A woman who'll take a risk to get it. You did nothing wrong last night, Kit. And neither did I. Listen, I don't need some strait-laced writer with a fear of authority writing my book. I need someone who isn't afraid to be herself. To let herself go. To wonder. To ask. To kiss. To fuck.'

I say nothing. I can't tell if I'm flattered or annoyed. He kissed me to find out if I'm a slut? Okay. Great. I guess for someone to write a book about his particular product, it makes a sad amount of sense.

I stomp sullenly down the stairs, Ian at my heels. When we reach the bottom, he stops in front of another door. It's massive, heavy-duty, and armored. It's intimidatingly important-looking, like the kind of doors I imagine they have in bank vaults.

Ian turns to me. 'Are you ready to meet him?'

A shiver rolls down my spine, my moodiness dissipating all at once. I can't help myself from beaming up at Ian. Finally, I get to meet him. The reason for the book, the reason I'm here. The elusive, the elite, the most sought-after luxury item in the world: Eros.

I've never been more ready for anything in my life. Eros is the tech advancement that has changed how we work, how we live, how we view computers as a whole. There are entire offshoots of philosophy, of ethics, based around Eros. There are even rumors of a cult that sprang up recently just to worship him.

'Yes. *Yes*. I'm so fucking ready.'

Ian grins, typing a code into the security interface, and the door unlatches. It opens, slowly, sliding from right to left. And then we step inside.

We're standing in a wide, well-lit corridor. Like the stairwell we just came down, it's bland and grey, a nondescript length of cement floor and dreary walls. The only thing breaking up the monotony are sections of wiring against the wall, like intermittent waterfalls of wire from floor to ceiling.

'Welcome to my lair,' Ian says, spreading his hands wide.

'It looks like a hallway,' I say for the benefit of my recording.

Ian laughs. 'You're not afraid of me, Kit. I like that. A lot of people are.' He turns to me. 'Did you really want to fuck me last night?'

I freeze, startled by the question. I hesitate, wondering if there's an answer he's looking for. But I decide there's no reason to lie. 'Yes.'

He gives me a long look, his eyes roaming across my body without any indication of self-consciousness. 'Good. You'll like Eros.'

If I weren't about to meet Eros, I would be losing myself in speculation about Ian's plans for future drunken makeouts. But I'm too overwhelmed with anticipation, vibrating with excitement and nerves.

I've seen Eros of course. On television, in ads, even from very far away at certain high-security exhibitions downtown. But Eros isn't for people like me. He costs more than a private jet and requires far more upkeep. I did plenty of research to prep for this. I know everything there is to know about Eros – everything available to the public, that is.

And maybe . . . if the book does really well, if I'm really lucky, one day, I could even afford my *own* Eros.

'And here we are,' says Ian, stopping before a door marked with four letters in all caps: EROS. 'Only one

Eros lives with me. The rest are off-site. The great majority of testing and manufacturing takes place in my factories and labs.' He smiles at me, his glasses gleaming in the fluorescent light. 'You're about to meet my first successful Eros.'

'What did –' I begin, as if I'm going to ask a coherent question. But all thought flees when Ian opens the door.

All I can do is stare. The room is smallish and entirely white. A white circular dais graces the center of the floor. And standing casually on the dais, in the mode of Michelangelo's David, is a young man with curly golden hair and smooth tan skin. A gauzy white toga drapes pleasingly from his angles.

He is Eros.

There is nothing to differentiate him from a statue. He doesn't move, he doesn't breathe. He's the most beautiful thing I've ever seen. It's like they took the most perfect parts of every ideal man throughout history and legend and combined them into one. He's Alexander the Great. He is both Achilles and Patroclus. He's Apollo, beautiful and terrifying. He is the god of love himself.

Ian glances at me, and for the first time, I see a hint of eagerness in his gaze. Like he's finally allowed to be vulnerable here, at the feet of his holy child. Like he's finally allowed to hope that he made something good.

'How do you like him?' Ian asks.

I lick my lips. My mouth has gone dry. 'He's beautiful,' I whisper. 'Perfect. I thought . . . well, I've seen him before. I know what he looks like. But it's not the same, is it? In person. Every pore, every strand of hair, the veins in his arms . . . It's so intimate.' I move forward, almost by instinct.

'You may touch him,' Ian says. 'He's in sleep mode. Nothing you do or say will be picked up or remembered.'

'What, you don't want him hearing all this praise?' I say laughingly. 'Worried he'll get a big head?'

Ian moves up to run a hand along Eros's well-muscled thigh. He gazes up at his creation. 'The more he gets to know you,' he says, 'the better he can please you.'

A shiver rolls through me. I imagine what it must be like, having your own Eros. I wonder how he arrives. In a box? Do you unpack him like any other parcel, setting aside the cardboard and the Styrofoam until you reach his muscular warmth? I wonder if he needs to be lifted from the packaging, dead weight until he's ready to be turned on.

I imagine him watching me, learning me, understanding me. And when I need him, he already knows what I want.

Does he also know what to say after? Does he murmur sweet nothings? Does he clean you up and kiss you goodnight?

'I want to say hello.'

'Everyone does,' Ian replies, rolling up his sleeves. He crouches, pressing something at Eros's heel. Then he stands, arms crossed.

A ripple rolls through Eros. It's almost imperceptible, maybe even imagined, but I'm sure I can see him come to life. He's a statue one moment, and a human the next. He's soft, malleable, and breathing. His chest rises and falls. His fingers flex. His nostrils flare on an inhale.

And then he opens his eyes.

His gaze flits to Ian, and then to me. He smiles slowly, like a lover just waking up in the morning after a long night of making love. I don't believe Eros ever fucks. He makes love. Those long musician's fingers, the sensual lips – those are an artist's features. And sex must be his canvas.

'Good morning, Katherine Fox.' Eros's voice is warm, like summer sunlight on the Mediterranean Sea.

My heart caves in.

When I was a kid, before my parents disappeared from my life, they took me to Italy. We visited a cathedral where monks still sang every evening at Vespers. I remember staring up at those stained glass windows, wondering if this was what it felt like to believe in God.

That's how Eros's voice makes me feel.

He's not human. He's a machine. From his well-formed feet to the curls on his head, he's utterly synthetic. Those eyes, which seem to look through me and into the very depths of who I am – they're mechanical. Every magnificent part of him is fake, manufactured, invented.

But I feel I'm in that cathedral again, looking up at God's image and *almost* believing.

'How do you know my name?' I ask.

Eros steps off the dais and moves toward me. His movements are smooth, unmarred by human imperfection. He lifts his hand to cup my face. His skin is warm, and his touch is gentle but confident. I can't help but melt into him.

'I know all about you, Katherine Fox.'

'I updated him before you arrived,' Ian clarifies. 'Uploaded all your info. It's wireless, of course. He doesn't need Bluetooth. No wi-fi necessary. That's another thing we're working on – integrating tech that doesn't cut out, that isn't exclusive from device to device. Imagine if individual Eroses could speak to each other, receive instructions without needing me to upload data. The possibilities! Endless. Endless.'

'Wow,' I say, staring up at the Pleasurebot. His hand still cups my face. His gaze is sweet, his brows arched over bright blue eyes. There are absolutely no flaws. No hints that he's inhuman. He's fucking *perfect*. I feel like a whole new world just opened up before me.

'Katherine Fox,' says Eros, 'how are you?'

'Call her Kit,' Ian says, coming around to stand beside me. 'She prefers Kit.'

'I'm sorry,' says Eros, dropping his hand. He smiles, bright as the sun. 'Kit.'

Ian turns to me. 'Want to fuck him?'

# 5

The question takes me off guard. 'Oh, no thanks. I'm good for now.' Not that I wouldn't gladly, but I'm a little shocked by the brazenness of Ian's offer. Eros is right there. He can hear us.

Ian shrugs.

I wonder if Eros is offended by the question. Or is he excited? Does he care? But of course he doesn't. He's a Pleasurebot. He's artificial. Every emotion on that face was pre-programmed.

'I'll send him up to you later if you want,' Ian says. 'You can't leave without sampling. Eros will make you come so hard you cry.'

'Talk about pull quotes,' I say, half-laughing, trying to ignore the way my body responds. 'I'm putting that in the book.'

'I'll give you better sound bites,' Ian says, waving a dismissive hand. 'We're just getting started. You hungry yet? I'll make breakfast.'

Eros seems to understand that his meet and greet is over. He returns to his dais with elegant steps, and I can't drag my eyes away. He moves like a dancer, every muscle taut and poised. He assumes the David pose, but when Ian bends to press the spot on Eros's heel, my chest constricts.

'Wait.'

Ian turns to me with a questioning look.

'Can he . . . Can Eros join us for breakfast?' I smile at Eros; I can't help it. He smiles back. 'For the book.'

Ian straightens, eyeing me. 'He can't eat.'

'That's okay. I'd just love to speak with him. To see your dynamic.'

Ian turns to Eros. 'You want to come to breakfast?'

Eros's smile broadens. 'I would love to join you for breakfast, Kit.'

I grin back.

'Yeah, yeah, all right, let's go. Come on.' Ian makes for the door, pausing to let me go through first. He and Eros join me in the hallway, Eros looking comically bizarre in that cement-grey corridor with his gauzy toga and golden skin.

Ian closes the door behind us. 'So, Kit, you like him?'

I glance at Eros, then back at Ian. 'Of course I like him. Is it . . . I mean, he knows we're talking about him. Does he mind? Eros, do you mind?'

'I don't mind,' Eros says.

'He doesn't mind,' Ian repeats, pushing his glasses up his nose. 'Right, Eros? You don't mind. You want to fuck Kit later?'

'Jesus, Ian –'

48

'It would be an immeasurable honor,' Eros says, taking me by the hand. He gazes into my eyes like a lover. I have to look away; the strange sweetness of his gaze almost hurts.

We head toward the vault door, back the way we came. Our footsteps on the concrete floor echo in discordance – my slippers and Eros's sandals, softly padding; Ian's bare feet, slapping almost obscenely on the hard, cold surface.

We approach a door that hangs an inch or two ajar. I don't remember passing it on the way to Eros's room. It's dark inside, though I can see what I think is a shadowy shape, elegant and tall.

'Ah,' Ian says, sidling over to the open door. He shoots me a tense smile as he pulls the door closed and locks it with a quickly typed code. 'Ignore that. A prototype. Very new. Unpredictable. Disobedient.' He chuckles, moving past the now-locked door. 'Eros is more your speed. He's got wide appeal, completion guaranteed. Completion guaranteed.' He rolls his shoulders, hands in pockets. 'Isn't that right?'

'You will always achieve an orgasm with me,' Eros says, polite as anything. 'I'm extremely skilled.'

'I'm sure you are,' I say, trying not to titter like a schoolgirl. I'm finding it hard not to react to Eros as if he's a human. He looks like one, sounds like one, acts like one . . . but he isn't. And I have to keep reminding myself that this is an interview for a book, not a personal fun day at the Pleasurebot factory. I need to be asking probing questions. 'Ian, do you offer refunds if Eros doesn't deliver on that promise?'

Ian barks a laugh. 'Sure, sure. If he doesn't get you off.'

'Has anyone ever asked for one? A refund.'

'No. Never. Eros delivers. He always delivers what he's programmed to do.' Ian's expression turns strangely cold. 'No surprises.'

'And the prototype?' I ask, glancing back at the now-closed door. I like the sound of it – unpredictable. Disobedient. Those words spark a little flame in me, an eager curiosity. What would it mean for a Pleasurebot to defy orders? 'I assume it comes with no guarantees.'

Ian turns to face Eros and me, walking backwards down the austere corridor. 'No, no, no guarantees. *He* is not in circulation yet. Might never be. I'm testing new tech with the prototype, faster neural pathways. A new physical look, ethereal, exciting. But I'm still testing. And I think he'll be –' he cuts himself off, smiling slowly. 'You've got me talking against my own judgment, Kit. Yammering away. You have a gift! Doesn't she have a gift?'

Eros nods. 'Yes, Ian. Kit is easy to talk to.'

'But what exactly do you mean the prototype is unpredictable?' I persist, drawn to that shadowy form, the being I glimpsed for just a moment. 'How can that be? He's a computer program.'

Ian waves a hand. 'There's a software bug, a glitch that makes him . . . disagreeable. Sometimes angry. I haven't found the pathway responsible. He doesn't comply with my tests. But that's the point of him! To obey.' He laughs. 'So I shut him down indefinitely.'

'He sounds fascinating.' A million questions claw at my chest and throat, begging to get out, my curiosity overflowing. I can't remove that image from my head, the glimpse of the prototype, a slender shape in the darkness. 'For the book,' I say, 'wouldn't it be possible for me to –'

'Kit,' Eros says, his hand falling warmly on my shoulder. 'What's your favorite breakfast food?'

I glance at Ian, who smirks. 'He's inquisitive. He has to know you before he can fuck you properly. If you want the full experience, he needs to know all about you. Answer his questions. You'll thank me later.'

A sudden arc of desire pulses through me from my chest to between my legs. I close my eyes for a long moment, willing my body to relax. Do I still have blue balls from last night? God. 'I love pancakes,' I say, replying to Eros's question. 'With a side of bacon.'

'Salty and sweet,' says Eros. 'I like that.'

Ian snorts.

Ian starts making breakfast while I watch from the kitchen island. I notice with an embarrassed sort of delight that he's making pancakes and bacon. Eros hovers nearby, assisting when Ian asks. Eros's movements are practiced and easy. He seems to be just as elegant in the kitchen as he's purported to be in bed.

Even Ian seems to be at ease; he and Eros move around each other with practiced familiarity. There's a rapport between them.

I sip a fresh coffee and wonder why Ian keeps Eros in that vault all alone. They know each other. If I didn't know better, I might think they're friends. I think of Eros alone in that dark room, and even though he's not human, even though he isn't conscious . . . It seems cruel.

Ian slides the first batch of pancakes onto an oven-warm plate.

'Eros,' I say, 'are you comfortable?'

He turns to me. 'Of course I am, Kit. Thank you for asking.'

'I mean, your . . . toga,' I persist, eyes fixed on his muscular bare legs, his knee-high sandals. I know I'm being silly, but I can't help it. 'Aren't you cold?'

Eros smiles. 'I'm not –'

'He's fine,' Ian interrupts, turning to face me, brandishing a spatula. 'He doesn't feel cold, he doesn't feel hot. His temp is regulated from the inside. He'd actually overheat if he didn't have fans and heat sinks. Eros, are you cold?'

'No, Ian.'

Ian raises his eyebrows. 'There.'

Breakfast is simple and unfussy, laid out on the kitchen island along with a pot of coffee, a carton of orange juice, and a glass bottle of pure maple syrup. Ian and I each take a stool. Eros stands on the other side of the island as he watches us, smiling blandly.

I'm about to invite him to join us when I remember he doesn't eat. I chew uncomfortably, feeling awkward about this mechanical audience that feels so deeply human.

Ian seems completely unconcerned about Eros's presence or lack thereof, prattling on about his high-rise, how he had it built to his personal specifications. He says something about ley lines, which piques my interest for a few minutes before my attention slides back to Eros. I want to ask him about himself. I want him to ask *me* questions. As much as I admire Ian, for just two seconds, I want him to shut the fuck up.

'They're geomagnetic,' Ian says, taking a bite of pancake and washing it down with orange juice. 'But stronger, more intense, better vibrations. We're right on a hot spot. Right on it. Everything I do is for a reason, Kit. Everything has thought behind it. I'm not a fucking idiot; I don't create just for fun. I don't do it for money. I don't do it for ego. I do it to *learn*. To *discover*. The prototype, for example –' He cuts himself off, smiling slyly at me. 'Now, now, you've got me talking again!'

'Why won't you tell me more about the prototype?'

I ask, my curiosity rising. 'I'm under NDA. I can't tell anyone under pain of death, or whatever the contract says.'

Eros's gaze darts between Ian and me.

Ian smiles slowly, but his eyes are dark. 'The prototype isn't up for discussion. It's top-secret stuff, still in development.'

'But –'

'You wouldn't like him anyway,' Ian cuts me off. 'The prototype is not like Eros. Not easy, not simple, not pliant or sweet. Isn't that right, Eros?'

Eros nods. 'Yes, Ian. You wouldn't like him, Kit.'

But I think I almost see hesitancy in Eros's expression, a stiffness in his jaw that wasn't there before.

'The prototype has his own personality,' Ian continues, chuckling. 'A bad one. I don't know why I keep him around. He'll never change. He's unfixable.'

'He sounds like most of my exes,' I quip, unable to help myself.

'There's one thing the prototype *can* do,' Ian says, holding my gaze, 'that I'm confident none of your exes could.'

The look in his eyes makes my skin heat. 'Oh?'

'Just like Eros, the prototype is godlike in the sack,' says Ian. 'He's a Pleasurebot through and through, I made sure of that. It's the most important aspect to me, you know. The most important. He was supposed to perform *better* than Eros, more attuned to his partner's wants and needs. Eros can make you cry? The prototype will make you swear off sex with humans altogether. He'll ruin you.'

I drop my fork. It clatters loudly on the plate. 'Sorry.'

Ian smiles slowly. 'You have me talking again, Kit.'

'Good,' I say. 'That's what I'm here for. But Ian . . .' I glance at Eros, whose expression remains utterly impassive but for the odd twitch of the jaw. 'Are you *fucking* your Pleasurebots?'

He throws his head back, his Adam's apple bobbing with laughter. After a few moments, he gathers himself, then shakes his head and peers at me shrewdly. 'You're funny.'

I turn to Eros. 'Well? Is he?'

Eros smiles back but says nothing.

'Ian,' I persist. 'You just said the Pleasurebots' sexual performance is important to you, which makes sense. And, forgive me, Eros, but you're . . . *they* are a product. They're being tested in some way, right? So *someone* has to be fucking them.'

Ian sips his coffee, watching me through long, dark lashes. 'Tell me what you're getting at, Kit.'

I swallow. 'I'm not getting at anything. I'm asking questions. For the book.'

'You want to fuck Eros?'

'I –'

'We've established that you want to fuck me.'

'Ian, this is –'

'So maybe you want to fuck us both.'

I purse my lips, pressing my thighs together self-consciously as if that will subdue the coil of desire growing there. Ian's eyes are dark, his beard thicker than yesterday; he hasn't shaved. He smells like rain and musk. Eros seems to glow, even in the fog-heavy gloom, pinks and blues of neon ads playing off his partially revealed abs.

'I'm not sure I . . . I'm not sure I'm comfortable having sex with a robot,' I manage.

Ian turns on his stool to face me, and in one smooth movement, he wedges his knee between my legs, parting them. My heartbeat skyrockets. Just like last night, he lifts my face with his fingers, his thumb pressed to my chin. He leans in slowly, and just like last night, there's plenty of time to stop this. I *should* stop it. I'm here for work. And there's a Pleasurebot watching us this time.

'Say the word,' Ian murmurs, leaning so close his lips brush mine, 'and I stop. But I think you want this.'

I remember the way his kiss felt last night. Competent, practiced, sensual, intoxicating.

Fuck it. I close the small distance between us.

He deepens the kiss almost immediately, his tongue seeking to undo me. His kiss tastes of coffee and sugar. He makes me want to forget how insane this is.

*I should stop this*, I think, as I moan into his mouth.

*I should stop this*, as he buries his fingers in my hair.

*I should stop this*, as he hooks an ankle around my stool and pulls me even closer.

I'm gasping by the time Ian breaks the kiss, and aching for more.

He raises one hand, snapping his fingers. 'Eros.'

Shame lances through me at the realization of what I'm doing. That this mechanical man has been watching me make out with his –

But the thought judders and disappears forever when Eros moves around the kitchen island and, without pausing or hesitating, comes up behind me and kisses my neck. His hands slide down my sides with slow, aching precision. His mouth is soft and insistent against my tender flesh. I arch back against him, closing my eyes, hating that Ian is here too, that I'm doing this, the same thing I always do – giving in.

# 6

'Good, Kit,' Eros murmurs in my ear, sweet and encouraging. One of his hands flattens against my belly, warm and firm, his fingertips reaching just beneath the waistband of my jeans.

And then another pair of hands is on my body, rougher, palming my thigh as if to hold me steady. Ian. I'm grateful for the anchor. I feel like I'm about to fly apart at the seams. Ian's other hand drifts upward from my waist and under my sweater, thumb caressing delicate circles against the skin of my ribs. I gasp when he teases at my nipple, the barest hint of pressure against sensitive skin.

Then Ian kisses me, swallowing my gasp. The sensations are almost enough to make me combust: Eros's mouth on my neck, his fingers under my waistband, inching lower. Ian's thumb pressing, teasing at my heaving breast.

I buck my hips into Eros's hand, whining against Ian's mouth, aching for more touch, more pressure.

'Shh, be patient,' Eros says, biting my earlobe. It's the most beautiful earlobe bite I've ever experienced.

It's like he knows exactly where to access the most pleasurable nerve endings. My eyes still closed, I feel him flick open the button of my jeans, lowering the zipper. 'We'll get you there.' His voice is deep, sensual, devoted, and it drips over me like honey.

The rain picks up and thrums against the window. I let them do what they want to me, following their hedonistic lead.

Eros's fingers find their way beneath my panties. Ian pushes up my sweater with practiced ease, Eros ceasing his kisses just long enough to let Ian pull the sweater up and over my head. I'm not wearing a bra. Ian's mouth finds my bare breasts. His tongue finds my nipples.

In a wanting, desperate haze, I feel Eros depart from my side. I miss him, wanting that mouth, those hands – until Ian picks me up and carries me into the living area, setting me down in front of the sofa. Eros is sitting there already, naked and waiting.

In a second I'm naked too, Ian's hands making quick work of my jeans and underwear. And then Ian is encouraging me, caressing me, ordering me with hot words in my ear to sit on Eros's cock.

Eros's stomach muscles ripple as he lifts his hips to invite me to him; his erect cock so human, so thick and taut, it makes my mouth water. There's even a pearl of precum glistening at the tip.

A Pleasurebot can't possibly be so perfect. But there

he is, watching me with an indecent gaze, his golden hair mussed and hanging in his eyes.

'Kit,' Eros croons. 'Come here.'

I climb willingly into his lap. He takes my waist in his large hands and kisses me. I thought Ian's kiss was good, but Eros's mouth is otherworldly. He was built for this. Programmed *just* for this. No, not for this – for *me*. Every touch is a spark of code, an electric communication from me to him: *This is how to touch me, this is how to kiss me, this is how I like it.*

Eros drags me closer to him, my cunt leaving a wet trail along the side of his erection. My breasts press against his firm chest, and I groan. He feels so human. His body, his movements, everything he does is flawless.

'Kit,' Eros says, nuzzling my neck, his chest rising and falling against mine. 'Bite down on my shoulder.'

'Why?' I whine, rolling my hips involuntarily, already aching, dying to come. All he's done is kiss me; all he's done is sit me against the length of his hard, waiting cock, and I'm already begging for it. All I want is to feel him inside me. I want to come until I'm crying, just like Ian promised.

'Do what he says,' Ian orders, and I remember hazily that he's still behind me, still watching, voyeuristic.

Eros lowers his head to my chest, licking a nipple with a languid tongue. I anchor my fingers in his hair, the sensation sending wavelengths of pleasure jolting through me.

'Because,' Eros says, 'this might hurt.'

I don't question. I want it. Whatever he's going to give me, I want it.

I clamp my teeth on his shoulder, and he even tastes like salt, like human skin.

And then Eros grabs me by the waist, lifting me up a few inches and adjusting himself, and slams me down on his cock until he's deep inside me.

I bite him hard, my cry muffled against Eros's skin. The sensation is so intense I almost black out, but it doesn't hurt. Instead, it's *overwhelming*. Almost *too* good. Like I've never been filled like this before, fucked so matter-of-factly and so precisely. It's like he's not reading my mind; he's reading my *body*.

He's bottomed out inside me. Just like I wanted. I'm almost afraid to move, afraid that it will send me over the edge too soon.

Then rough hands grab me from behind, one tangled in my hair, the other reaching over my shoulder to massage my breast. Ian pulls my head all the way back until I'm gazing up at him, breathing hard, exposed, and shaking with unspent ecstasy.

Ian is still fully dressed. He kisses me roughly, awkwardly from this angle, and then he slides his hand down to between my legs where I'm joined with Eros, my cunt full and aching. He presses a finger to my clit, and I gasp, the sound of a desperate woman.

'Ride his cock,' Ian growls in my ear.

He loosens his grip on my hair enough for me to find a good angle, but he remains pressed against my back, his hand at the nape of my neck, a low sting at the roots of my hair where he's pulling.

It's an easy order to obey. I roll my hips slowly at first, feeling out this new lover, getting a sense of his girth inside me, which angles work best. But God — *every* angle works best. I move in small circles, and I feel like I'm ascending. I bounce high, slamming his pelvis against mine, and it's a miracle of pleasure. I'm at the edge of orgasm, the heady, breathless edge of the fall, for what feels like hours. Years.

Eros touches me exactly where I need it, kisses me when and where I want it. All meaningful thought flees my mind, and I'm a figment, an electrical impulse, ricocheting from obscene ecstasy to decadent rapture.

Ian's fingers are still pressed firmly on my clit. And then he circles me once, slowly.

'Come for us, Kit,' says Eros.

I whimper, every muscle in my body taut, as I crest the wave.

'Now,' Ian orders.

So I do. And when the seemingly endless drowning pleasure subsides, when I can think and breathe and see again, Eros strokes my cheek so softly, so sweetly, that I can't hold it in anymore. Tears slide down my face, a desperate release.

*Fucking Christ.*

'Good,' Eros breathes, holding me to his chest. 'Beautiful.'

'That was fun,' Ian says, voice low and husky. I turn to look at him, Eros still deep inside me. Ian is rock-hard and breathing heavily, his pupils large and dark. 'You enjoy that?'

I did. God help me, I enjoyed it. 'Yes.'

He licks his lips. Then he looks away, and I'm not sure he's even talking to *me* anymore. 'Good. Good. It gets better every time with Eros.' He glances back at me, brows drawn low, and a shadow flickers across his expression. 'He'll never be the prototype, but he's still spectacular.'

And then Ian stalks away, toward what must be his room, and disappears down a corridor. I wonder if he's going to jerk himself off now. *I* would if I were him. I wonder if he has a voyeur kink, if *this* is how he tests the Pleasurebots.

And most of all, I wonder, if *this* is what it's like with Eros . . . what the fuck would it be like with the prototype?

Alone with Eros and suddenly self-conscious, I slide off his cock. It springs out of me, still hard. I hurriedly pull on my clothes. Eros only watches, and I swear his expression is . . . it's almost like he's enjoying it. But he's programmed for that, to look eager. To look hungry.

I pause while fastening my jeans. 'Eros,' I say, 'do you . . . I mean, did you want to –'

'No, thank you,' he says, languidly fisting his cock. 'I could help myself if I wanted to. But I'm satisfied. You make the most delicious sounds when you come.'

For a second, I'm lost for words. My face must be turning bright red. 'Oh, um. Thank you. Uh, listen, I need to go clean up.' I gesture vaguely toward the staircase leading up to my guest room. 'Are you okay alone for a few minutes?'

Eros nods, standing. I drag my eyes away from his cock. 'I'll clean myself up, Kit.'

'Okay. Thanks again.'

'You're welcome.'

Overcome with a sense of surreality, I hurry up the spiral staircase. I'm almost to the top when Eros speaks, stopping me in my tracks.

'Kit,' he says. He sounds almost pained. I lean over the railing and meet his gaze. He looks — strange. Almost sad, or . . . some emotion I haven't seen on him. Which program is this? I wonder. The one where he apologizes that my orgasm was somehow subpar?

But he says nothing.

'What, Eros?' I prompt.

And then, like a window closing, Eros's furrowed brows even out, his smile returns, and he shakes his head. 'I don't know. I forgot what I was going to say.'

# 7

Back in my en suite, I head straight to the shower. I'm sticky with sweat, and I smell like sex. Who knows how long Ian will be busy doing . . . whatever it is he's doing. And Eros said he'd be fine on his own down there, so I decide to take my time.

I shed my clothes and climb into the shower, turning the water up as hot as it will go before it scalds, and stand in the hot stream until my heart returns to its normal rhythm.

I take a long, steadying breath. There's nothing wrong here; I did nothing wrong. This isn't like the time I accidentally fucked a married guy. Ian is famously a bachelor. This isn't like the countless times I've fucked a near stranger while drunk, either. I'm fully sober. I just had pancakes, for God's sake. And Eros isn't a stranger. He's . . . well, he's a sexbot. He's built for this. It's his *purpose*.

Still, I feel unsettled.

'Best sex of my life, though,' I say aloud to the shower.

And better than that, it's incredible content for the

book. If Ian lets me, I could turn this into a chapter of its own. 'Testing the Pleasurebot,' or something. I'll come up with a better chapter title when I'm not sex-stupid, but who *wouldn't* want to buy a book with a first-person account of what the original Eros model is capable of?

I dry myself off, suddenly excited, all my unease dissipating in the shower's steam. It's hitting me little by little: the reality of this. I just fucked a *real-life robot*. And I'm going to write a book about it. A guaranteed bestseller. I'll be rich. I'll be fucking famous.

Pulling on my clothes, hair still wet, I feel clean and refreshed inside and out. I feel competent, satiated, *light*. I pull my hair into a bun, knowing it will dry in nice, loose curls that way, and grin at myself in the bathroom mirror.

Something catches my eye in the reflection. Movement in the room behind me.

I freeze, adrenaline spiking through me.

It was probably just a shadow, a drone passing by outside, silhouetted against the window. The lights are off in the adjacent room, and the curtains are drawn, drenching the corners in near blackness.

I turn away from the mirror.

There is a shape just inside the closed door of the guest room. At first, I don't understand what I'm seeing. It looks like a dark shadow, floating or hovering.

Wait, no.

It's an arm. A long arm, reaching *through* the door from the hallway outside. Slow and shadowed, seemingly unhindered by the door in its way, it reaches for me with outstretched fingers.

And then it flickers. Lines and spots of white skitter across the shape. At the same time, a heaviness grips me, and I feel like I'm being pulled down through an impossibly tight tunnel, every cell of me crushed flat. My vision darkens at the edges.

Then the arm's fingers seem to lengthen, to curve toward me.

Heart in my throat, I reach for the bedroom light switch.

I flick the light on.

The shape is gone. My room is empty.

I slump against the bathroom doorframe, my heart thudding like a jackhammer. It was just a shadow, a trick of the light. This crazy altitude. Maybe even some fucked up vibrations from Ian's ley lines, making me see things.

'I need to chill the fuck out,' I announce to no one.

I take a minute to gather myself, and then I'm hurrying down the spiral stairs to rejoin Eros. But when I get to the foot of the stairs, I see that I'm alone. Eros is gone, and Ian is still, apparently, jacking it in his bathroom.

I meander to the kitchen, refilling my now lukewarm cup of coffee. I could use a stiff drink, but it's still a little early for that. Closing my eyes, I pinch the bridge of my nose. It's still a little early for a devil's threesome with a Pleasurebot, but that didn't stop *me*.

The rain is picking up. I watch as it lashes the window, rivulets of neon-bright water coloring the glass. The storm has made it so dark that the city's lights are on early, and it feels like midnight rather than early afternoon. There's a heaviness in the air, a vibration that feels like waiting. Like an anticipatory inhale, or the pulse of silence just before a lightning strike.

Shivering, I turn away from the view. I much prefer the sight of Ian's home, austere as it is. It's warm and quiet, and I don't like looking out that window.

I take another sip of coffee.

'You imagined it,' I say aloud, trying to dispel this strange mood, to regain the sense of excitement I'd had in the shower.

It wouldn't be the first time I hallucinated, I rationalize. Once, I spent a month microdosing mushrooms under the impression it would improve my mental health. But the girl who'd sold them to me didn't mention they were mushrooms she grew in her own cellar, a detail that would have been nice to know beforehand. As it turned out, these mushrooms were not remotely safe for human consumption, and I was lucky I'd only been taking minuscule doses. Even so, I saw a lot of fucked up, nonexistent things that month.

Whatever I saw back in my room, I'm determined

to put it out of my head. I'm more than ready to get back to the tour and back to work. Back to not being alone at the top of a skyscraper.

I wander into the living area, nervously sipping my coffee. Where did Eros go? How long is Ian going to fuck himself for? Did he fall asleep? Maybe he's taking a shower too.

Then something catches my eye. Something that I'm pretty sure wasn't there before: a piece of paper on the bar. The back of my neck prickles as I approach.

It's a note. Written hastily, almost unreadable:

*Off-site lab emergency. Back soon. Make yourself at home. — Ian*

Off-site lab emergency? Right after a mind-blowing three-way and my horrifying hallucination? Okay. Sure. Great timing. I'm alone in a Pleasurebot house of horrors.

'It's not a house of horrors, Katherine,' I scold myself, going around to the other side of the bar. I rummage around until I find the bottle of whiskey Ian was using last night and pour a healthy amount into the remains of my now-cold coffee. 'You're safer here than some random guy's apartment. Ian's *lawyer* knows you're here.'

I take a sip and wince at the burn. It's early to start drinking, but I already feel better, knowing that in a few minutes and a few more sips, I'll be loose and relaxed, hopefully enough to think straight. I figure Ian brought Eros back down to the vault before he left. Maybe I'll even have time to get some writing done.

Mug in hand, I head back toward the spiral staircase, thinking I'll retrieve my laptop from the guest room and hang out down here, maybe draft a list of specific questions I'd like to ask Ian. Now that I've spent time with Eros, I'm starting to think of more specific things I can ask him, too. Maybe I'll even start on a loose outline for the book. The narrative concept is already taking shape in my head.

I pause at the foot of the stairs and swallow the last of my coffee, a nice little buzz beginning to fizz its way through my veins. I glance over my shoulder, my gaze falling on that nondescript door in the far wall, marked only by a keypad.

I think of that shadowy form in the vault below.

I remember Ian's words: *The Prototype will make you swear off sex with humans. He'll ruin you.* Ian wouldn't have said that if he didn't want me interested. He wants me to find out for myself. Deep down, he *wants* me to meet the Prototype.

Anticipation buzzes on my skin.

I head toward the door to the vault, setting my empty coffee mug on a side table on the way.

Ian talks a big talk. He flatters; he tells me my blog is so innovative and brilliant. He claims to see me as an intellectual. An equal, even. He picked *me* over every other writer in the world. But I know he's full of shit. Because he didn't cover the keypad when he was typing in the door codes. And I'm always paying attention.

'He wants something groundbreaking,' I murmur, stopping to stand before the nondescript door. I type in the keycode. 'I'll give it to him.'

# 8

After typing in the code, I tense up, expecting the panel to refuse me. Like it can read my fingerprints or my DNA and will set off an alarm or electrocute me. But nothing happens. And then, with a click, the door unlocks.

I enter the cool, dark stairwell.

I flick on the lights, and the door closes behind me.

My belly thrills with the knowledge that I'm going behind Ian's back. That I'm acting out. That I really am about to do this. It *has* to be what he wants. He's been pushing me toward this all day. He wants me to have some depraved sexual experience with the Prototype, just like I had with Eros. Maybe he's hoping to burst in on us, some kind of cuckolding thing. I hope not. That would be too weird, even for me.

Aware that Ian could return at any minute, I thunder down the stairs as fast as I can go without falling and breaking my neck. My curiosity flits to his mysterious offsite lab emergency, wondering what kind of emergency could possibly require Ian's help. But as I descend, moving deeper into the belly of Ian De Leon's stronghold, my thoughts return to the Prototype.

*Disobedient.*

I shiver with fear and excitement.

What does that *mean*, exactly? Is he cruel? Aggressive? Does he force himself on unwilling partners? Does he try to engage them in endless conversation instead of getting straight to the act? I giggle nervously. It echoes through the stairwell, reverberating back to me, a mad little chuckle.

My footsteps echo on the stairs, muffled by my slippers, and for a second, I feel like I'm entering the Underworld, and the Prototype waits for me as Hades himself, the god of this place.

I pause at the bottom of the stairs. The imposing vault door looms before me. The air down here feels heavy with anticipation. Like the whole universe is holding its breath.

My chest tightens. I really shouldn't be here. I should not have come down here.

A distant, muffled sound catches my ear.

It's coming from inside the vault door. The noise crawls toward me like a nightmare in slow crescendo. At first, I think it's the wind. But it's too deep for that, too guttural. And then I realize it's a wail. A long, drawn-out, unearthly cry.

I step backward by instinct, every cell in my body telling me to turn and run back upstairs. Back to warm light and a well-stocked bar. I could make another drink and wait for Ian to return. I could leave this place, these sounds, alone. I *should* forget this.

But I can't.

The wailing pauses for a second, and then it continues, louder. A low banging rises alongside the wail, metallic and violent.

Something sounds like it's slamming against one of the doors down here, over and over.

My throat closes up.

But I move forward, step by step, until I'm standing at the vault door.

'Don't be a pussy, Katherine.' It's the pep talk I give myself when it's late, and I'm drunk, and a strange man offers to take me home. When some girl I barely know sells me a bag of unidentified dehydrated fungi. When I see the pendulum about to swing back toward me, but I don't want to get out of the way. I willingly let the blade eviscerate me, millimeter by millimeter, and I don't know how much skin and muscle is left before I'll break wide open, spilling my guts on the floor.

I type in the key code.

The wailing gets louder and louder. The slam of what could be a body against the wall, over and over, over and over.

The door unlocks, and I push it open.

Everything goes silent. The wailing stops. The metallic slamming stops.

I stand on the threshold, my breathing shallow.

'There, see?' I whisper. 'All in your head.' Or it

was the wind or some strange weather phenomenon. Maybe when I opened the door, it changed the conditions. Maybe it's the fucking ley lines talking to me.

Either I go through the door, or I don't.

'Katherine. Suck it up.'

I step through the door.

Even though my heart skitters in my chest, even though there's a knot in my throat warning me of danger, nothing happens. I'm just standing there, shaking like a deer in headlights, while nothing happens.

My body is lying to me. There's no reason for all this anxiety. It's quiet down here. Perfectly safe, like it was earlier when I was here with Ian. And those horrible sounds were just like the shadowy arm in my room: nonexistent.

Time to meet the Prototype.

My thoughts, eager to be distracted, fill with that shadowy shape in the dark room. The elegance of him. I wonder how he'll look, how he'll sound. If he'll let me touch him.

Up ahead, I see Eros's room. I have the strange urge to go up to the door and press my ear to it. I'm sure he's back inside. Could *he* have made those sounds? Could he be . . . broken or upset? What if he wasn't turned off, and he panicked in the dark? I wonder if Pleasurebots ever feel frightened or confused. If *I* woke up suddenly, locked in a dark room, I would probably scream and pound on the door, too.

No sound comes from within Eros's room.

'Eros?' I whisper, knocking lightly. I'm afraid to speak any louder, like something unwanted will hear me.

He doesn't respond. Of course he doesn't. He's in sleep mode. The thought of him standing in that room, beautiful and still as Michelangelo's David, hidden away from the world in utter silence and darkness, raises a sudden lump in my throat. He should be outside. He should be enjoying his youth, or . . .

I pull away from the door abruptly. There is nothing Eros *should* be doing. He's fine. He's a complex program loaded onto some very sexy hardware. I may as well be lamenting the fact that my phone can't get married and raise a family.

And Eros isn't why I'm down here, anyway.

My breathing is still shallow. A sweat breaks out on my upper lip as I turn to the door that hung ajar earlier. *His* door. The Prototype.

The wail, those echoing slams, reverberate in my mind. I'm shaking. Fight or flight wells up in my chest, demanding that I flee.

*Don't be a pussy, Katherine.*

Every minute that goes by is a minute that Ian could return. That those strange sounds, the vision in my guest room, could become real and cause me harm. But I don't stop. My feet carry me forward. I have eyes only for that door.

I type in the code, and there's a soft click as the door unlocks.

Every hair on my body stands on end. My stomach flips, fear and excitement turning my gut to mush. I push on the door.

I hold my breath.

Darkness waits for me beyond. But as the door swings open, pale light fades on, slowly brightening to illuminate the room. It's just like Eros's: empty and white, but for a circular dais at the center. And on the dais, unmoving, bathed in shadow, stands the Prototype.

His features are shadowed. He's tall and elegant. Unlike Eros, he is not posed artfully, but stands unassuming, his weight distributed to one leg, the other bent slightly at the knee. His arms are folded in front of him. His face, mostly obscured, seems peaceful in the darkness.

I step into the room.

The light brightens just enough to clear the shadows from his face.

My heart stops.

The Prototype is breathtaking. Where Eros is bright and vivid, almost *more* than human, this . . . this creature is something else. His skin is pale porcelain, so smooth and delicate that I can see his synthetic veins running like blue threads underneath. Thick silvery hair falls past his shoulders in waves. His nose is angular, aristocratic. Cupid's bow lips turn down to meet a sharp jaw and chin. Dark, elegant brows arch low and brooding over honey-colored eyes.

Every part of him is beautiful, making up an achingly flawless whole. But a shadow seems to hang over him. His expression is almost dour. And his clothes, intricately embroidered black pants and shirt, vaguely Medieval in style, reveal nothing but his throat, face, and hands.

There is nothing other than his physical attributes, and maybe the reputation Ian has so effectively crafted for him, to set the Prototype apart from Eros. But *I* feel infinitely different. When I saw Eros for the first time, I was overcome with awe, eagerness, fascination. But with the Prototype, here and now, I feel like I'm taking the final step of a long and arduous journey. I'm breathing fresh, unspoiled air for the first time.

It's strange, almost embarrassing, reacting this way to a silent and unmoving figure. Strange that my heart has slowed to a tranquil crawl. My muscles have relaxed, my shoulders slumped in a palpable relief. Strange that from the moment I stepped into this room and saw the Prototype, I felt a bizarre, inexplicable sense of comfort.

It doesn't make any sense, but I go with it. Better strangely calm than strangely disturbed.

I make one full circuit around the Prototype, blatantly admiring him one last time before we meet. And then I kneel at his feet, pressing the back of his heel. He's wearing boots, but through the supple leather, I feel something give way. I scramble to my feet, stepping back. I don't want him to be startled when he wakes.

I hold my breath.

Slowly, like the first wind of a brewing summer storm, he comes to life.

His extremities shift first, moving hesitantly, testing. Then he inhales. Exhales. The sense of comfort, which I begin to recognize as deep familiarity, washes over me like a sun-warmed sea. I watch his every move like I'm trying to memorize him.

And then his eyes alight, and he blinks, turning slowly to look at me.

The world falls away.

For an instant, I feel like I'm tumbling from the top of this skyscraper, rain-lashed and free, until the world opens up and a silent blackness envelopes me, welcoming me home.

And then the feeling goes as abruptly as it came. I'm lost for words, for understanding. What the fuck is this Pleasurebot doing to me?

All the while, he watches me, wordless and sharp-eyed. Like he's assessing me. Reading me. Knowing me until I'm stripped naked before him, until skin and muscle are pulled away, until I am nothing but bone and sinew, until that's gone, too, and I'm a bright and pulsing energy.

I can't hide from him, even if I wanted to.

'Hi. Sorry to wake you.' My voice wavers.

The Prototype tilts his head, and his mouth softens. 'Hello.'

His voice hits me in the chest and coils all the way down to between my legs. It's deep and knowing, and it fills me up like thick, honey wine. Immediately, I know he's nothing like Eros. He's winter and Eros is spring. He's a god while Eros is nothing but a faithful priest. And somehow, I feel so acutely, so intensely, down to the core of my heart and in the cells of my makeup, that *I know him.*

'Please don't apologize,' he says. 'Thank you for waking me.'

'You're welcome,' I whisper. It's the most I can muster.

The Prototype steps from the dais, slow and digni-fied. He is long-limbed and slender, taller than Eros. He approaches me in what feels like slow motion. Every movement plays like a kaleidoscope before my eyes, bright and unending and terrifyingly unreal.

*I know you.*

And does his gaze reply? Does he see it in my eyes; does he know me too?

He draws closer, his hair falling behind his shoulder on one side to reveal a pale, corded neck. The embroi-dery on his shirt winks in the soft light as he moves, and I see the rise and fall of his chest, the shift of muscle beneath.

God, what a gorgeous achievement of engineering. I swallow hard. He's mechanical. He's a program. *A program, Katherine.*

'May I ask your name?' he says, halting just outside my personal space. His gaze is firm and earnest, and I can't look away.

'Katherine Fox,' I answer. 'But . . . you can call me Kit.'

He reaches out to tuck a stray piece of hair behind my ear. 'Kit,' he says.

My name has never been spoken like that – like I'm known. Needed. *Cherished.* His fingertip brushes my skin, and it feels like an electric shock. I only just manage not to lean my face into his hand like a cat, purring with pleasure.

When he withdraws, his soft skin no longer touching mine, I feel a sense of unspeakable loss. After a moment of silence, I realize it's my turn to say something.

*Do I know you?* I want to ask.

It's on the tip of my tongue, ready to fall out, when I catch myself. What kind of stupid question – of course I don't. And I *don't* know him. Fuck. What is *happening* to me? I inhale sharply, trying to pull myself together.

'Do you have a name?' I ask.

He smiles. It's fleeting, but it hits me like an arrow in the heart. That smile catches hold of every one of my

84

anxieties and crushes them to dust. That smile is the most lovely thing I've ever seen. It's like coming home to a place I've never been. It hurts to look at him.

'Orpheus,' he answers. 'My name is Orpheus.'

# 9

'Did Ian give you that name?'

My chest hurts. I imagine him down here all alone for who knows how long, locked away in the dark. Ian said he had been shelved indefinitely. I can't even wrap my head around the concept of the Prototype – of *Orpheus* – being down here, silent as a statue, *forever*. He's too perfect to be hidden away.

'Yes,' Orpheus says. 'Ian named me.' He glances down at the floor, then back to me. His eyes narrow slightly, like he's thinking.

I feel suddenly ill. All the ads say Eros is not sentient. He is not a true artificial intelligence but is built to mimic it. *True* AI doesn't exist yet. Because if it did, we would have to ask a lot of questions about what it means to be human. And if we took it a step further, Pleasurebots could no longer be classified as products. They would be slaves.

Suddenly, Ian's questions from last night don't feel hypothetical at all.

Because Orpheus is not like Eros in the slightest. It's not just the way he speaks, the light in his eyes, the subtle flickers of expression across his face. It's that he elicits more emotion in me than Eros does, more than he should.

'Do you like your name?' It's an incredibly boring question, but I find that I'm desperate to get on some kind of firm, normal footing with him.

'It will suffice.'

'Do you have any other names?' *Names I might recognize?*

He gives me a long look. 'No. Do you?'

I laugh, a self-conscious, nervous giggle. He's intoxicating. On top of this feeling that I know him, everything he says, every movement, elicits an emotional response. 'Yes. My middle name is Elizabeth.'

'Beautiful,' he breathes.

A flash of desire flickers down my spine, a lightning strike of need. I lick my lips. I'm losing it. 'It's boring. Every other girl my age has that middle name.'

His mouth lifts in an almost imperceptible smile. 'Just because a thing is common doesn't mean it's not beautiful.' The smile fades. 'But Kit, you are not common.'

I take a deep, fortifying breath. 'Well, neither are you. You're different, aren't you? Different from Eros. You're not the same type of . . . I mean, you're . . .' I falter. I can't help it; I have to know. 'Orpheus, I'm so sorry, this is going to sound insane, but I have the weirdest feeling . . . have we met before?'

Suddenly, Orpheus is right up in my space. He moves like a shadow. He gently takes my face in his hands, tipping my head back so I'm still holding his gaze. His brows draw together. 'You found me.'

For a second, the statement doesn't register. I'm overwhelmed by his closeness. He smells . . . he smells of a distant place, a far-off thought. And if he kisses me, which I suddenly and very desperately want, I worry I'll start crying.

'Ian was giving me a tour of the facilities,' I explain. 'I'm writing a book for him. This door was open earlier, and I saw you. I wanted to meet you.'

Orpheus wipes a thumb across my cheek, and I realize I *am* crying. I should be embarrassed, but Orpheus's closeness, the concern in his expression, has rid me of all self-consciousness. He takes the tear-wet thumb and presses it to his mouth, licking off the salt.

'I'm glad,' he murmurs, his other hand still holding my face.

'Glad to meet me?'

He strokes my jaw with his thumb, a low sound of approval rumbling from his chest. 'Yes,' he murmurs. 'Very glad to meet you.'

My eyes flutter closed, and this time I *do* finally break and lean my head sideways, pushing it into his hand, groveling pathetically for more. 'Ian told me you were a prototype model,' I say, eyes still closed. 'That you don't work correctly.'

His thumb's rhythmic movement stops for a breath. 'I am disobedient.'

I open my eyes.

Orpheus's gaze holds mine, and he frowns, studying my face as if trying to make sense of me. 'Do you want me to be obedient?'

'No.' *I want you exactly the way you are.*

'Do you want me to behave myself?'

'No.' *Unless you want to.*

'Do you want me to pleasure you, as this body was built to do?'

'No.' *It wouldn't be enough.*

He inhales sharply and then stills. 'Then what do you want from me?'

I don't want what Eros gave me. Physical pleasure could never be enough, not from Orpheus. I want to *know* Orpheus. I want to understand him. I want to experience him in a way that transcends simple touch.

'Nothing,' I answer. 'I don't want anything from you that you aren't willing to give.'

*Because you're more than a fucking Pleasurebot*, I don't say. *Because you light something up inside me that has never been lit before.*

But I don't have the guts to say it. Because it sounds insane.

He kisses my forehead, sweet and delicate. In my delusional mind, I imagine that he's confirming, silently, that he understands everything I didn't say.

'Thank you, Kit.'

'For what?'

'Wanting nothing from me. No one has done that before. Not here.'

I open my mouth to ask what that means – *Not here* – when Orpheus lifts his head, gaze sharpening. He steps back from me, leaving me bereft, his gaze locked on something beyond the room. 'Ian is coming,' he says. 'He'll be home soon.'

My stomach jolts, and I plummet back down to reality. I don't know how long I've been down here, playing imaginary love games with a Pleasurebot. 'But how do you know –'

'I know,' Orpheus says. 'He's coming.'

'Okay,' I breathe. 'Fuck, I have to go. I have to turn you off. I'm so sorry.'

But Orpheus is already on the dais, taking the same pose I found him in. He inclines his head. 'Put this body to sleep, Kit. I'll see you again soon.'

Anguish fills my chest. Ian won't get an emergency call every day I'm here. 'I don't know if I will –'

'I'll see you again,' Orpheus repeats.

I nod, swallowing a sob as I kneel at his feet. I've only just met him, but it feels like I'm losing a loved one.

I press the back of his heel, and then he's gone.

Already, that sweet, familiar feeling that's been holding my heart in a caress is beginning to fade. Everything seems sharper now, colder.

I turn for the door, knowing that, barring any cuckolding sexual proclivities, if Ian finds me down here, he'll have me thrown out. The book will be canceled. But just before I slam Orpheus's door shut behind me, I turn and look back.

He stands unmoving on the dais.

I shudder at the sight, and bile rises in my throat. Like this, he's no longer Orpheus. He's the Prototype, nothing more than a marvel of engineering. It's like looking at a corpse.

I close the door and type in the code. The lock clicks, and I'm sprinting down the corridor, back through the vault door, and up the stairs. Over and over as I run, one thought repeats itself: *He's a fucking robot, Katherine.* Whatever I met in that room was a program inside an enticing body, all engineered by Ian De Leon. Orpheus is a Pleasurebot, programmed to seduce human women. He's probably *programmed* to make everyone around him feel secure, familiar. Maybe it's a frequency he emits, a psychological trick, a hypnotic effect.

*He's a fucking robot, Katherine.*

I only just make it back up to the penthouse, lungs on fire, legs aching, when the elevator pings. I know how breathless I look, my cheeks flushed, hair in disarray. I rush to the sofa, flopping into a sitting position, trying to look casual.

The doors slide open.

Ian clocks me immediately, and our gazes lock. I think he narrows his eyes for a split second, some unknown emotion tightening the edges of his mouth. But then the moment passes.

'Fucking Christ,' Ian huffs, a sigh and a curse, going straight for the bar. 'What a day, what a *day*. Sorry to leave you high and dry.'

'No problem.' I'm relieved to find that I sound almost normal – not too obviously winded from jogging up several flights of stairs. 'I've just been brainstorming for the book. I came up with a slightly new direction.'

He rummages in the bar, pulling out a crystal glass and the whiskey. 'Yeah? Tell me.'

'I have ideas. I mean, it's a biography, but what if I put essays and slice-of-life anecdotes between each chapter? I think the public would love it. I'm thinking maybe I can include some of my personal experiences. From here in the penthouse.' I don't have to elaborate; it's obvious what I mean.

'Sure, sure.' Ian's response is distracted, dismissive. He pours himself two fingers of whiskey and turns to face me, leaning his elbows on the bar. His dark eyes are piercing, the planes of his face softly lit with blue and purple from the alternating lights of a high-rise ad outside.

From where I watch, Ian looks almost inhuman. The contrasting light playing across his features, the way his hair falls just so, long black lashes framing a steady gaze. It's like there is a sheen of unreality between us, or a canvas on which he's been painted, and I'm trying to connect with a truth that can't be seen.

I think of Orpheus, the connection I felt between us, the hint of obsession. I've experienced something like it before. I mean, I know who I am – I've been horny and infatuated too many times to count. But with Orpheus, it felt different. More. It was an intoxicating ache deep in my chest, more than just lust. And I hate that I feel empty without it now, that I miss it, that I miss *him*.

Ian watches me intensely, sipping his whiskey. Unspoken words spark between us, and I wonder how much he assumes. Does he guess I met his gorgeous creation in the vault? Does he see the wiring of my heart trailing away and down the stairs, down to where Orpheus stands unmoving in the dark?

'You should have a drink,' Ian says, joining me on the couch, his whiskey already half-gone. 'You look pale.'

Rain drums the window, filling the taut silence between us, the breath before I speak.

'I'm fine.' I'm acutely aware of my posture, the tone of my voice. He's watching me, reading me. 'Did you take care of the emergency?'

Ian eyes me. He takes a slow sip of whiskey. 'I did.'

'I hope everything's okay.'

'It is.'

94

'Good.'

He holds me in his gaze for a moment longer, then turns to the window, staring out at the drenched cityscape, its neon lights like cybernetic stars. 'I hope you made yourself at home while I was gone.'

'I did.' Even those two words feel like an admission of guilt.

'And I hope you know that you can be comfortable with me, Kit. Honest. We're friends. I thought Eros and I might have made that clear.' His words are laced with levity, but his jaw is firm, his heavy brows unyielding. 'You can talk to me.'

I bite the inside of my lip, remembering Ian's tongue in my mouth, his fingers between my legs. 'I appreciate that. Thank you.'

He's quiet for a moment. Then he says, 'Eros loves the rain. It fascinates him. It's new to him. It wasn't part of his programming at first, weather events. He understands people, our emotions, our needs. But he doesn't understand the world. He used to stand at this window and watch the sunset. And when it rained, he'd ask how it felt. The water on his skin. He wanted to know if it was hot or cold. If it would burn. If it tickled. He never found out. Not this model. I built him here, you know. Right here.' Ian jabs the sofa with a forefinger, still staring out at the rain. 'He never left this penthouse. He never will.'

'Did you program him for that?' I ask.

Ian turns his attention back to me. 'For what?'

'Yearning. For what he can't have.'

A shadow flickers across Ian's face. 'Yes. Yes, of course. Everything is programmed. Every voiced thought is not a *thought* at all. It's a program.' Bitterness infuses his words as he speaks. 'It's all a trick, a novelty, a simulacrum of humanity.'

I don't know what to say to that. Ian's mood seems to be darkening by the minute. Whatever happened at his lab must have been worse than he's admitting. As I watch, he downs the rest of his whiskey, stands abruptly, and heads for the bar. A traffic drone's lights pulse through the window, lighting the room in soft orbs of flashing red.

Ian pours himself another drink, downs it in one, and slams the glass on the bar.

'I'm done for the day,' he says. 'I'm tired. I'm done.'

'But I'm just getting started,' I protest, sitting up straight. 'I have so many questions.'

'I said I'm done for the day,' he snaps. And before I can stop him, he stalks away into the one hallway I haven't been down, the one that leads to his room. I hear a door slam.

Everything is quiet except for the sound of rain on glass. And I wonder, for a second, what the fuck I'm actually doing here.

It's two in the morning, and I can't sleep.

I spent the rest of the evening in my bed, staring at a blank Word document and nibbling on a stale protein bar I found at the bottom of my suitcase. I should have eaten a real dinner – my stomach churns in the dark – but that's not what's keeping me awake.

Over and over, the memory of Orpheus plays in my mind: his elegant movements, the vibration of his voice in the deepest, most unknown part of me. The thought of him envelops me. I close my eyes, and it's like he's *there*, waiting for me, beckoning me to him.

I toss and turn, even the sound of the rain doing nothing to soothe me. The night weighs heavy and presses on my lungs, threatening to suffocate. I roll onto my side, resting my hot cheek on my outstretched arm, the pillows long since flung from the bed. It's so windy the rain angles across the window, blown in solid sheets. Condensation blurs the glass, turning the city into a million spots of color. I can almost feel the building sway in the wind.

What would happen if I fell from this height? Would

my body fall apart from the seams as I plummeted? I have the insane urge to leap from the bed, fling open the window, and toss myself out. Like the abyss is calling to me. Like it could wash me clean and make me anew.

'Go to *sleep*,' I plead with myself, squeezing my eyes shut. 'Go to sleep, Katherine.'

But Orpheus's voice rumbles back at me from the darkness.

*I'll see you again soon.*

Sudden pressure on the mattress jolts my eyes open.

A black figure looms over me, half propped on the bed, staring with gleaming yellow eyes.

I open my mouth to scream, and a cool hand clamps over my mouth. The sound dies in my throat.

As soon as he touches me, I know.

What I thought was a demon-yellow gaze fades to soft honey. My eyes adjust to the dark, and there he is: one knee propped on the mattress, his body curved over me as if in protection, his hair falling around us like a silver waterfall.

He removes his hand from my mouth.

'Orpheus,' I gasp. 'What the hell? How are you here?'

He stares down at me. 'I missed you.'

I prop myself up on my elbows and slide backwards, needing to get a better look at him, to understand. He was *asleep*. Did Ian change his mind and send him up here?

Orpheus remains where he is, one knee propped on the bed, shoulders hunched, animalistic. 'I told you we'd meet again.'

'But you were . . .' I whisper. 'I thought I . . .'

'You thought you turned me off?' he finishes for me. 'What you and Ian understand about me couldn't fill a thimble.' His voice is low and hypnotic. He crawls fully onto the bed, the weight of his body pressing divots into the mattress as he moves toward me.

My breath hitches with anticipation. I've been wanting him all night. I've been restless in these sheets, imagining his weight on me, his mouth on my skin, wishing he were here. Now he is, and I can't help but wonder if I summoned him here to me, if my yearning was so acute that I willed him into my bed.

'I could also say the same of you,' Orpheus continues, looming over me. His hair glows bluish in the light. 'You have hidden depths, Kit.'

My body feels pulled to his, magnetic, inevitable. I'm barely following his words; I'd much rather fall into him and abandon my thoughts altogether. 'What do you mean?'

'You already know, deep down.' He reaches for me slowly, running one knuckle along my jaw until he brushes my ear. 'I'm sorry if I frightened you.'

I shiver, a needy exhale falling from my lips. The world spreads out around me, soft and cool, as if I'm floating in a still ocean, my head cradled by soothing waters. The beat of my heart, the roar of blood in my ears, the rain on the windows, the traffic drones – everything grows quiet. Everything drops away.

There is only him.

'You didn't frighten me. I was hoping you'd come.'

'Good,' he says. 'You never need to fear me.'

'You never answered me before,' I say, reaching for him, burying my fingers in the hair at his nape. It feels right for me to do this. Natural, instinctual. 'When I asked if I knew you.'

His lips are inches from mine. 'There are ways for souls to meet that have nothing to do with distance. I've been watching you for years. I've been calling out to you. And now, in this place, you can finally hear me.'

My brain short-circuits, stuttering to a momentary halt. What the fuck is he talking about?

Orpheus presses a gentle finger to the wrinkle between my furrowed brows. 'Think of every beautiful dream you've ever had. Dreams that felt like home.'

I swallow a lump in my throat. 'But how does that . . .'

'You felt that you were looking into some faraway, inaccessible place. Some beautiful world that wasn't real.'

My arousal is fading fast, replaced with wariness, confusion. 'You lost me.'

'You asked if we knew one another. The answer is yes. You have heard my voice, filtered through the sunlight of your dreams. You have seen my face, hidden in the shadows of your nightmares. And I have watched you for a long time. You are rare. You are perfect.'

Then he kisses me. It's a lightning strike. I become nothing but energy, pure uncut sensation, as his mouth softly caresses mine. Like I'm a billion filaments of light, skittering along the universe's infinite wiring.

My mind slows with every second that passes. He lowers his body to mine, my hips rising up to meet his.

*Fuck it.*

I'll ask questions later. Right now, I need Orpheus. In every possible way.

I curl my hands around his neck, pulling him down. He finally settles his full weight on me, letting out a breath as he slides an arm under me, gathering me against him. Sparks of need flicker along my body everywhere we touch – his hand at my back, my breasts against his chest, his erection grinding down against me where I'm hot and wet.

Every sound, every movement, feels so good I want to die. His lips against mine are a revelation of ecstasy. His hands on my hot skin plot the course to a pleasure I've never accessed before. His tongue opens up worlds of desire.

Orpheus feels so incredibly human. But the sensation rising in me, the pleasure expanding in my chest and down to my core, is more than that. It's more than anything I've felt before. I've never been so *consumed* like this. Eros was perfect like fireflies on a summer night. But Orpheus . . . Orpheus is perfect like a ferocious storm, cleansing and terrifying and unavoidable. Orpheus doesn't just understand what I want – he gives me what I never thought I needed.

Rain drums on the window. The neon night pulses around us, muddled through foggy glass and raindrops, softly lighting the bed.

His hands roam over me, feather-light. He caresses my breasts with a transcendental mouth. He murmurs unintelligible words into my skin until I shiver, goosebumps forming where his lips graze me.

'Do you want to fuck me?' I ask, breathless. It feels like such a silly question. Fucking is the least of what I want from Orpheus. But right now, I'll take whatever he wants to give me.

'I don't want to fuck you, Kit.'

A knife lodges in my chest. 'You don't?'

'You don't want something as simple as to be fucked,' he says. 'You want more. You *deserve* more. And I can give it to you.'

I arch my back as he kisses my breasts, my head angling back into the mattress, my eyes fluttering closed. 'But do *you* want . . .' the breathless words catch in my throat. A fleeting, faraway thought comes to me: He's a Pleasurebot. *Wanting* isn't part of his design.

But the thought flashes and dissipates like a blown fuse. Orpheus is nothing like Eros. Eros is a melody, but Orpheus is a symphony. A sublimely sonic dream.

'I want to make you come,' he says, propping himself up on both elbows. His soft gold eyes hold me, his hair reflecting a cascade of city light. He's painted in color, ethereal but solid. He feels infinitely safe. 'I can make you come in ways you've never imagined. You thought you knew pleasure before you met me. You were wrong. I'll show you what ecstasy truly means.'

Electric desire crackles down to my core. I need his mouth on every sensitive part of me, his hands all over me, his cock inside me. 'Show me. Do whatever you want with me.'

He smiles, a slow, almost melancholic curve of the mouth. 'With you, what I want is simple. I want to give you *everything*.'

He lowers his hand to my belly, softly caressing his way down, down to where I need him most. And with one curve of his fingers, he's inside me, and I'm nearly undone.

His breath tickles my ear. 'Say my name.'

'Orpheus,' I gasp, arching under him.

'Again.'

'*Orpheus*.'

The night surrounds us, fading into slow pleasure until the rapture of his touch is all there is. *He* is all there is.

He is everything. And he gives himself willingly.

'Ian told me you like the rain. Is that true?' I sip my coffee, relishing its heat, the bitter taste.

'That is true,' Eros answers, alert and bright-eyed. He leans toward me, smiling a little, his elbows braced on the kitchen island. 'The rain is very romantic.'

Ian turns around from where he's fiddling with the coffee maker and shoots me an inscrutable look. His curly hair is sleep-mussed, and dark circles hang heavy under his eyes. My gut twists at the wild intensity of his gaze. 'Eros is a goddamn flirt,' he says. Then he returns his attention to the coffee, and the tension dissipates. 'Next time you fuck, it'll be even better than yesterday.'

I shift on my stool, crossing my legs. I can't deny that it's crossed my mind. But the memory of Orpheus looms large, distracting me. I'm here for the book. For my *future*. But Orpheus gave me so many orgasms last night that I lost count. And when I woke up at half past ten this morning, instead of leaping out of bed to catch up on time lost, I just laid there for another half hour, wishing Orpheus was still with me. He had vanished just as stealthily as he'd appeared, sometime before dawn, leaving me wanting more.

Eros watches me patiently, waiting for my next question.

I came down from my guest room to find him here already, helping Ian in the kitchen. I've been asking both man and Pleasurebot pointed questions since I got up, trying to make up for lost time. Ian is in a mood, his answers either monosyllabic or almost sarcastically wordy, like he's trying to piss me off. And there's a darting, high-energy vibe to him that puts me on edge.

'Kit,' says Eros, startling me out of my thoughts. 'Do you like the rain? Wait –' he smiles. 'I think you do. I see the way you look out that window. You're a romantic, like me.'

I study his sweet, open face. Eros is intoxicatingly beautiful, golden and vivid against the backdrop of Ian's home, but he's lost something since the last time I saw him. A glow, a sheen. I've seen Orpheus now, and I've fucked them both. Eros can't compare.

'I do love the rain,' I answer, smiling back despite myself. Eros is still a ray of sunshine, even in this dreary weather. 'Is that a trait Ian shares?'

Ian hands me a fresh mug of coffee. I hadn't even noticed him taking the empty one from me. My mind has been up in the fucking storm clouds.

'We are nothing alike,' Ian grumbles, going into the living area to face the window, his back to Eros and me. Silhouetted by the view of rainy Los Angeles, he looks like some tortured leading man in a noir film.

Eros and I lock eyes. He raises his eyebrows, the corner of his mouth twitching. 'We do share some traits,' Eros admits. 'We both love gazing melodramatically out windows.'

I laugh, delighted by the joke. 'Did Ian teach you that?'

Eros frowns slightly, tilting his head. 'Teach me what?'

'How to be funny.'

Ian snorts. 'It's a natural side effect.'

Eros glances at Ian, then back to me. His expression is suddenly shadowed, like the sun drifting behind a cloud.

'A side effect?' I repeat. 'Of what?'

'Of being trapped in here with me,' Ian says in a low voice.

Eros shrugs, smiling. 'Ian is very funny. I've learned so much from him.'

But I don't think that's what Ian means.

Ian sighs, turning away from the window. I watch as he goes to the bar, pouring two glasses of whiskey. He returns to the kitchen and hands one of the glasses out to me. 'Go look at the rain or something,' he says.

I hesitate.

'Not you,' Ian says, his sharp tone scraping at my nerves. 'Eros. Eros, go look at the rain.'

'I would love to, Ian.'

I watch Eros turn and stride to the wide window, his muscles flexing and stretching as he moves. His toga is so thin, so anachronistic, that it puts me on edge. I'd wanted to bring him something more appropriate to wear, but when I suggested it earlier, Ian shot down the idea. I still can't help thinking Eros seems separate from us like this. A spectacle.

'Here,' Ian says, setting down the whiskey and sliding it toward me. 'Put this in your coffee. Take a break. Take a break.'

'I'm good.'

Ian shrugs, tossing his back in one swig. Then he downs my drink, the crystal glass clinking loudly against the marble countertop. 'Suit yourself.'

'It's beautiful,' Eros murmurs, seemingly to himself. He looks back over his shoulder. 'Kit, do you want to watch the rain with me?'

I move to join him, but Ian stops me with a hand on my shoulder. He shakes his head, making a face. 'Don't bother, don't bother. He'll try to recite poetry or something. It's fucking embarrassing. I don't know why I put poetry in the repertoire.'

Annoyance, and a little unease, tickle at the spot between my shoulder blades. Yesterday, Ian was proud and eager, ready to showcase his creation. He was practically gagging to share Eros with me. Today, it's like the sight of us pisses him off.

Eros is still watching me, his expression undeniably hopeful.

I pull away from Ian. I can't deny the compassion I feel for Eros, alone by the window. Staring out at the rain like that, he seems so tragically human.

Ian settles himself on the sofa with a fresh whiskey while I join Eros at the window. My stomach tightens at the view, at the memory of yesterday's episode of vertigo. But as I gaze out over the rain-lashed city with Eros, I feel nothing but slight apprehension.

'I don't mean to ignore you,' Eros says, smiling sadly. 'I enjoy answering your questions. But Ian asked that I watch the rain, so I did.'

'And you always do what he says?' I glance sideways at Ian.

Eros lowers his chin. 'Of course.'

'Do you *really* like looking at the rain, Eros? Or is it just part of your —'

'Obviously, it's part of his programming,' Ian snaps, audibly irritated.

'I do,' Eros answers, ignoring Ian's tone.

'What do you like about the rain?' I ask, also ignoring Ian. I'm curious to see if I can get Eros to explain the mechanism of his own programming. Ian gave him yearning. But does Eros see it that way? Does it *feel* like programming? Or is it as ephemeral and unknowable as a human feeling?

Eros frowns slightly, his golden brows drawing

together. 'I like the sound of it on the windows,' he says. 'But most of all, I like that it makes the city look beautiful. I imagine the buildings are in some other world. The rain makes everything blurry and distant. Rain is . . .' he pauses as if forming a thought. 'Rain is a window into a place that's far away.'

'Stop,' Ian grumbles, and I turn to see him waving a hand at us, grimacing. 'Stop, stop. Goddamn it, Eros, the woman asked you a simple question.'

'He answered it,' I protest. My heart flutters like a captive bird at Eros's words. He answered it beautifully. Like he really could appreciate the beauty he beheld, like it *touched* him.

'I'm sorry, Ian,' Eros says, the embodiment of contrition. He looks back at me. 'I'm sorry my answer was so lengthy.'

'No, I liked it,' I reassure him. 'What else do you enjoy doing?'

Eros smiles broadly. 'I enjoy whatever activity I am encouraged to take part in. Singing, poetry, dancing, kissing . . . all of it. Most of all, though, I've enjoyed making passionate love to you, Kit.'

I bite my lip, pulse speeding at the memory.

'That's more like it,' Ian mutters.

'That's kind of you,' I say quickly. 'I liked it too.'

I allow my gaze to travel over Eros. He's still beautiful in the ghostly light of the rain-dark city. But his beauty and his readiness to please no longer strike me like a dagger of longing. Even our sex doesn't seem as mind-blowing in retrospect. Under the shadow of Orpheus, Eros has diminished.

*Orpheus.* I think of his form in the vault, waiting for me, asleep in the dark.

'Let me know if you want to have me again,' Eros says, taking my hand gently, kissing the back of my knuckles, and letting it fall.

Ian makes a sound of disgust behind me.

I spin on him, exasperated. 'Are you good, Ian? You've been weird all morning.'

Ian stares back, swirling his whiskey. His eyes are glazed, unfocused from intoxication, and I realize he must have been drinking since before I got up. Those last two drinks just sent him over the edge. He snaps his gaze to the window, a muscle pulsing in his jaw. He's silent for a few moments.

'I used to keep him up here,' Ian says at last, 'in the penthouse with me. There wasn't a reason not to. He would return to his room at night, recharge, and then come up here in the morning. It was almost like he was a person.' He pauses to take a drink.

Eros listens in silence.

'Almost like he was my *friend*,' Ian continues. 'I was in awe of him, my creation. He's fucking beautiful, as you can clearly see. And polite. And agile.' A ghost of a smile flits across his lips. 'For a long time, he was my only companion. I could talk to him a little. But when it came to real conversation, to philosophy and quantum physics and the nature of . . . of *beauty*, or *life*, or what the fuck ever, he had nothing to say. He repeated bits of poetry or pre-programmed fucking niceties.' Ian's tone grows harsh, grinding out the words as he speaks. 'He was *boring*.'

'He feels like a person to me,' I say softly, realizing I'm no longer sure what I believe about these Pleasurebots. I remember the cries I heard in the vault. I remember Orpheus's voice, lapping at my mind, telling me he's been *watching me*.

Ian's gaze snaps to mine. 'He's a machine, a computer, dressed up in pretty skin and pretty clothes. Nothing but a mechanical whore.'

My breath catches. The word feels like a slap.

Eros's expression doesn't change. He's half-smiling, eyes trained on Ian, like he's politely absorbing every word the asshole speaks.

'But the way he talks . . .' I say, almost a whisper. I trail off, not sure where I'm going with this. Why am I defending Eros's humanity? I know what he is. And what does it matter? Who am I to discern the difference?

Ian scoffs. 'Ask him about the rain again.'

'Ian —'

'Ask him *again*, Kit. See if he's a person.'

I turn to Eros, apologetic. 'Eros, why do you like the rain?'

'I like the sound of it on the windows.' Eros tilts his head a little as he speaks, and the gesture is familiar. It's exactly the gesture, the same expression, he adopted before when he answered the question. 'But most of all, I like that it makes the city look beautiful. I imagine the buildings are in some other world. The rain makes everything blurry and distant. Rain is . . .' he pauses, a line forming between his brows, just like before. Like he's trying to think of what to say next. 'Rain is a window into a place that's far away.'

Everything about the response – his gestures, inflection, tone – it's all the same. I feel like I've rewound a video and watched it again from the beginning.

'See?' Ian says.

'Well of course he'd say the same thing.' I try to rationalize the strange sense of loss. It's as if Eros has become smaller, somehow, like his gleaming facade has flattened to become a two-dimensional image.

'You don't get it,' Ian says, shaking his head. His whiskey glass is empty. 'I couldn't bear it. Eros became hateful to me. I had to put him to sleep and lock him away. Seeing him traipse around like this, reciting meaningless garbage, it made me *insane*. It wasn't enough. It wasn't what I *wanted*, do you understand?'

'But I thought you were proud of –'

'No, no, no,' Ian cuts me off. 'Eros wasn't enough. He could have been so much more. And then one night . . .' Ian is staring out over the city again, slowly turning the crystal glass in his fingers like he's recounting a dream. Like he's *in* a dream. 'I stood by the window, looking out over the city. A low cloud hung over the ocean, and I watched it move over Santa Monica, then Hollywood. It drifted inland against the hills until it settled over this building, dark and heavy with rain. I looked out, and I saw a reflection of myself, and it was like I was standing past the window in the sky. A twin version of myself, gazing back from across a void. A man looking back at me from another world. And I knew what I was going to do next. I was going to open a door.'

Ian is silent for so long that I think he's finished speaking. And then he drops the glass, and it rolls, droplets of brown marring cream carpeting. His mouth twists. 'I thought it would be beautiful.'

I don't know how to respond to Ian's drunken ramble. And I'm starting to doubt that the book is ever going to happen if this is the kind of intoxicated nonsense he's planning to give me for the rest of my time here.

'Kit,' Eros says, stepping toward me. I turn and see that he's holding out a hand, palm up. 'Is there anything you need?'

He's still so kind, so open, even after hearing all that. I wonder what kind of punishment Ian has subjected him to, whether it's all been verbal or if . . . My stomach turns. 'No, thank you, Eros.'

'Take him back,' Ian says, muffled. He's slumped over on the sofa, chin pressed to his palm, fingers curled over his face. The glass remains overturned on the floor. Rain pounds the window. Light flickers over Ian, painting him blue, then indigo, then purple.

I open my mouth to ask what he means.

'Take him back,' Ian repeats. His voice is harsh now, violent in its animosity. 'I don't want to look at him anymore. Take him downstairs. The vault.'

Eros and I share a glance. I see my reflection in the softness of his eyes, my uneasy expression, the reaction to Ian's outburst. A silent beat passes. Then Eros turns away, heading for the door in the far wall.

Part of me wants to stay and confront Ian, to ask him what the fuck his problem is; why he's acting like this. But I don't think I want to be alone with Ian right now. So I trail after Eros, biting my tongue.

Eros surprises me by typing in the key code, but then I remember – he used to come and go from the penthouse as he pleased.

I follow Eros downstairs, feeling useless. He doesn't need me to guide him. He's done this before. He used to do this every night. So why did Ian ask me to babysit? Did he just want to get rid of me?

We're silent as we descend, and a heavy weight seems to hang in my chest, pulling my heart down. I can't name the feeling, aching and sore as it is, until we're at the vault door.

Eros types in the key code, then pauses at the threshold. He turns to me. 'You don't need to come with me. I can put myself into sleep mode.'

I imagine Eros walking down that stark corridor, his golden hair and skin diminished in the fluorescent lights. I imagine him bending to press that indent at the base of his heel and slowly becoming a statue again.

'Have you ever woken up in the dark?' I ask suddenly.

Eros gives me a confused look.

'I mean down here,' I say, my mouth dry. 'Have you ever woken up in your room and been disoriented? Panicked? Maybe even panicked enough to . . . I don't know, cry out or pound on the walls?'

'No, Kit,' Eros answers. 'That has never happened to me. It sounds horrible.'

'It does.'

We stand in awkward silence. Then I say, 'I'll walk you to your room. It's no problem.'

What I don't say aloud is that I don't like the idea of Eros turning himself off down here alone, abandoned, unwanted. The thought makes me sick to my stomach. I *also* don't say that I'm desperate to see Orpheus again. Even if Ian is still conscious after all that whiskey, he can't possibly miss me for a few minutes if I stop by Orpheus's room.

Eros smiles, but something about the expression feels off. 'Very well, Kit.'

It takes everything in me not to stare at Orpheus's

door as we pass. When we get to Eros's room, he types in the key code again. He opens the door, then turns back to me.

I startle at his expression.

His eyes are dark, his full lips drawn together. Tension radiates from him. I've never seen him like this before. His golden radiance is suddenly shadowed, twisted, malignant. I move to step away, but before I can, Eros reaches out lightning-fast to grab my upper arm. His grip is impossibly tight. I'm frozen in momentary shock, adrenaline spiking.

'Eros?' I manage. 'What's wrong?'

'Don't trust him.' He speaks through gritted teeth as if each word inflicts pain.

'Who?' My skin crawls. His hold on me starts to hurt; he's going to leave a bruise.

Eros's eyes widen, his lips curling back to reveal teeth bared in a grimace of pain. He looks wild beneath the fluorescent lights, a feral creature trapped in a cage. Suddenly, I'm afraid – not of this unnamed threat but of Eros himself. I remember how easily he lifted me onto his hard cock. He could kill me in countless ways with almost no effort.

'Don't trust him,' Eros repeats.

'Don't fucking trust *who*?' I splutter, my voice high-pitched.

A tear slides down Eros's stricken, pain-contorted face. 'Don't. Don't.'

117

'Eros, please, are you . . .'

But as I try to form coherent words, Eros's grip on me slackens. His arm drops. His expression falls neutral like a switch flipping. Then he tilts his head. 'I'm sorry, Kit. I think I was distracted. Did you say something?'

I stare back, dumbfounded. My skin prickles with fear, and I swallow dryly. Whatever the fuck just happened, I want nothing to do with it. I want out of this vault. 'Nope. Didn't say anything.'

Eros smiles. 'Good. Have a lovely night, Kit Fox.'

He crosses to the circular dais, bends over, and presses the back of his own heel. By the time he's in his proper pose, his expression is lifeless.

I close the door, taking care not to slam it. I lean my back against it for a few seconds, trying to catch my breath. I don't have to ask Eros who he was talking about. I was up there this morning. I saw the bitterness, the harsh looks, the cruelty that laced his words when he spoke about Eros.

*Don't trust him.*

He has to be talking about Ian.

## 12

I hover at the top of the stairs, my hand pressed to the door that will open into Ian's penthouse. If he's in there, I have to act normal. I spent the whole walk upstairs trying to convince myself that Eros malfunctioned, that he said something else. But I'm not sure I am.

Whatever Eros meant, I don't think Ian is a danger to me. No matter what he says when he's sober, Ian's behavior this morning made something very clear: he isn't kind to Eros. He locked him in a vault, seemingly indefinitely, because he couldn't carry a conversation the way Ian wanted him to. And now, I assume, he's taking it out on me.

But he wouldn't hurt me. His lawyer knows I'm here. My phone can be tracked. He's just a volatile, bitter alcoholic.

I open the door slowly, heart in my throat.

The living area is empty. Shoulders slumping in relief, I close the door behind me and scan the room. No Ian. Just the rain endlessly drumming the windows.

'Thank fuck,' I breathe, heading straight for the bar. I could use that whiskey after all. But as I'm reaching for the bottle, something stops me. A strange, muffled sound. At first, I think it's nothing, maybe the wind howling. I curl my fingers around the bottle.

I hear it again, louder this time – a low, drawn-out groan that crescendos slowly until it's a hoarse sort of wail. Not this shit again. The sound is barely loud enough to hear above the rain and my own heartbeat, but I'm sure I'm not imagining it. And it's coming from the hallway I haven't been down. It's coming from Ian's room.

That fucking does it. I grab the whiskey bottle, spin on my heel, and run for the spiral staircase. I scamper up the metal stairs and rush into my guest room, slamming the door behind me and locking it. Without pausing to catch my breath, I dive into bed – whiskey still in my arms – and pull the covers over me.

I lie curled up under the blankets in a fetal position, breathing hard. It's what I used to do as a kid when I was scared, when I needed to be alone. I'd curl up under the covers and close my eyes, and the rest of the world would fade away. But I still hear the rain outside, lashing these impossibly high windows.

After a few minutes pass and nothing happens, I start to feel ridiculous. What did I think was going to happen? Ian suddenly rushes at me with a knife just because his Pleasurebot malfunctioned? Because now that I've had time to think, I realize it had to have been a malfunction of some kind. Eros's whole demeanor changed when he said that. It wasn't part of his programming. It was a momentary system failure.

Sighing, I sit up, pushing the blanket off. I inhale cool air and stare restlessly out the window. I'm also certain I was overreacting to whatever I heard downstairs, but my nerves are still buzzing like live wires. I take a drag from the whiskey bottle, then I roll off the bed, shed my clothes, and head into the bathroom. I need to cleanse myself, both literally and figuratively.

The hot shower streams over my naked body like a baptism. Whatever I witnessed in the vault earlier, it's being washed away with every drop of water on my skin, every fortifying breath I take.

And the wail I thought I heard coming from Ian's room? The wind howling. It's been the wind every time.

I open my eyes to grab the shampoo.

A tall, dark shape stands with me in the shower. It's fuzzy at the edges, undefined, like a figure obscured by fog.

A scream grows and dies in my throat, my terror choking me. Instinctively, I throw myself backwards, away from the figure.

Its edges flicker, beaded with static, and it moves toward me.

The next thing I know, I'm slipping, scrambling to catch myself in the slick shower. One foot loses its grip and flails out from under me. For a split second,

I see my skull slamming on the edge of the tub and Ian finding me there in a pool of my own blood. But I catch myself at the last second, regaining my balance.

And by the time I'm firmly on two feet again, the figure is gone.

It was only there for a second. Like a shadowy, human-shaped glitch in the universe.

Nausea churns in my gut. I turn off the shower, grabbing a towel and drying myself as quickly as possible. It was the same as the arm reaching into my room yesterday. The same as the figure outside the building, standing in the rain.

I'm going fucking crazy.

I dress hurriedly in the same skirt I arrived in, a pair of old tights, and yesterday's sweater. Not bothering with my damp hair, I grab my recording device, shove it into my pocket, and get the hell out of my room. I'd rather be downstairs with a drunk Ian than in here with . . . *that*.

I clatter down the spiral staircase, half hoping Ian will be back on the sofa where I left him before I went with Eros to the vault. As if I could erase the last hour or so from existence. I wish.

The living area is still empty.

All at once, a wave of anger rushes over me, heating my skin. Who the fuck does Ian De Leon think he is? Inviting me here to interview him for his book, promising me a bestseller, and then taking none of it seriously? All he's done since I arrived is get drunk, initiate sexual encounters, act like a dick, and then disappear mysteriously. Meanwhile, I'm seeing fucked up visions and being subjected to a bizarre warning in the basement.

And I'm starting to feel like I should take that warning to heart.

'Ian!'

His name, clipped and bitter on my tongue, hangs in the air. But there is no answer. Not even a distant, muffled wail from his room like before. Because that was a hallucination. Because I'm *losing* it in this place.

I stand there fuming, wondering if I should just storm into Ian's room and demand that he get his ass out here and take this book seriously, but then something toward the window catches my eye.

I squint, leaning forward, not sure what I'm seeing. It's . . . a shimmer in the air like a migraine aura. But when I move forward, I see that it's not just in my vision. It's real. It's stationary, a glowing irregular shape between me and the window glass, roughly oval, about a foot tall and half as wide. It's like a tear in the fabric of the world. It wavers just below eye level like a heat mirage. But unlike a heat mirage, it's fractured and jagged-edged, and fully opaque. I can't see the window through it. Instead, its center seems to be crackling with a dark, colorful energy. Colors shift within the mirage, orderly in shape – squares, lines, checkered patterns – yet utterly chaotic in their movements. Like pixels on a dying monitor.

I take another step toward the mirage, entranced. Its kaleidoscopic colors blend together like a drug.

And then something inside me . . . *flickers*. A dislocation. A glitch. A crackle in my ribs, as if my bones are coming apart delicately at the seams. It feels horrifically wrong, and it *hurts*, but part of me is also crying out for more, begging to be pulled apart and dragged through the darkness, to be remade on the other side.

Like the sensation in the elevator. Like the windows, when I'm too close. I remember the feeling of the fall, the pressure. *If I can just get to the other side –*

My breath hitches. The mirage is gone. Nothing stands between me and the window, the curtains of rain sweeping across the glass.

I sway on my feet, putting a hand out to brace myself on the sofa. I press my fingers to the bridge of my nose and mutter a string of soft expletives. Enough with this *fucking* shit.

'Ian!' I shout again, my voice rough with adrenaline.

No answer.

I barely know what time it is anymore. The city has been rain-dark for days now. Surely, Ian needs to eat. He'll come out eventually. A distant siren shrieks, faraway and eerie, as if the city below is another world entirely.

'Ian, you fucking dick,' I repeat. But I'm already

heading to his room. I don't care how many terrors I just witnessed, I'm not about to waste an entire day of work just because Ian decided to get drunk and pass out.

I pause at his door, hand raised to knock.

Eros's strangled warning echoes in my head, stopping me short. *Don't trust him.* I hesitate. But there are only so many rational choices here. Do I really think Ian's own creation would turn against him like that? It's not like Eros is . . . well, everything he does and says is a program. I saw that first-hand. He can't be sentient. It *was* a malfunction.

I knock on Ian's door.

There's no answer.

I press my ear to the door, listening for signs of movement.

Nothing.

'Ian,' I announce, 'I'm coming in. Don't be naked.'

I'm surprised when the knob turns. I thought Ian would be the type to lock everything away, just like he does his Pleasurebots. But when I push open the door, I see why the room is unlocked. It's empty. The bed is a mess, blankets and sheets strewn about. Ian's clothes from yesterday are piled haphazardly on the floor. And Ian isn't here.

Other than the bathroom, there's one more room I haven't checked. I passed it on my way down the hall, assuming from its half-open door and dark interior that no one was inside. With nowhere else left to search, I return to the dark room and peek in, speaking softly. 'Ian?'

I push my way in, and the door catches on something soft. I look down and see piles of books all over the floor. Clutter covers almost every surface. There are bookshelves along the walls, a desk, and an ergonomic chair. Over all of this, papers and notebooks are stacked in comically large piles.

But of course, Ian isn't there.

I'm about to pull the door closed when I pause. Ian isn't here. And this looks like a study or an office. These are probably Ian's personal notes, his notebooks. I might find something about Eros. My pulse speeds. I might find something about *Orpheus*.

Ian would never let me put stolen information in the book. But it doesn't have to be *in* the book to influence the work. If I want this book to be a slam dunk, I need to know exactly what goes on in Ian's head, even if he won't tell me.

So I go inside.

## 13

A motion-sensing lamp fades on, illuminating the room in a warm glow. Still vibrating with adrenaline, I go straight to the desk, picking up papers and notebooks at random. But my eagerness quickly fades to frustration. None of this makes any goddamn sense. Ian's notes are either scribbled in unintelligible handwriting that I'm not even sure is in English, or complex math equations that make my eyes cross.

'Come on, Ian,' I mutter, riffling through a stack of notebooks. 'Show me something good.'

I flip through one of the thickest notebooks, but I'm disappointed to find yet another collection of unreadable nonsense in the form of Ian's shit handwriting. I'm returning the notebook to the desk when a slip of paper falls out from between the pages, fluttering to the floor. I bend to pick up the paper. It's thin and white, standard printer paper, folded over twice. I open it gingerly.

There, in the center of the paper, scribbled in a shaky hand, is what looks like a random shape. But I know this shape. I know the lines and dots inside it. I know those jagged edges.

It's the fucking mirage.

I swallow hard, flipping over the page, hoping for an explanation. A label. *Something*. But there's nothing else to see. Turning the page back over, I hold it closer to my face, searching it for meaning. And then I see another mark on the paper, way down at the bottom edge. A hurriedly scribbled note. And even Ian's handwriting can't obscure the two words that stare back at me: *Katherine Fox*.

A slow trickle of dread drips down my spine. Because that's not all. Below my name, in even smaller print, there are four more words:

*He insists on her.*

I read the note again. And again. What the *fuck*?

Heart in my throat, I fold up the paper and slide it into my pocket. Whatever the hell it means, I'll figure it out. I'll confront Ian about it, if I ever find the asshole.

Then I remember the note Ian left when he had an emergency at the external lab. I didn't even think to look for a note this time. Hurrying back to the living room, I check the bar, the kitchen island, every available surface. But I know in my gut I won't find another note. I would have seen it already.

So either Ian left me alone here without any explanation, or he went back downstairs while I was in the shower. Down to the vault.

My stomach twists.

This goddamn vault. The cold hallway looms large in my mind, and Eros's warning pulses like a neon sign. I don't want to go back down there, not alone. Not if Ian is there, drunk and erratic. I pause. But maybe . . . if I woke Orpheus . . .

A sick little thrill rolls through me. Whatever happens down there, Ian drove me to it.

I go to the door in the far wall. Muscle memory types the code in, and when the door clicks open, it's a beckoning call. I slip through into the stairwell and begin to descend.

I'm almost to the bottom of the stairs when I stop dead in my tracks. The vault door is open. *Ian*, I remind myself. Ian is down here. I should be relieved, but my body stays tense, my chest tight.

'Ian?' My voice bounces through the vault door and down the corridor, too loud.

No answer. I keep going.

By the time I get to the vault door, my hands are shaking. I feel like I've hit my fight or flight quota for the day. Any more scares and my heart will give out.

'Ian?' It's only a whisper, but it feels like a shout. It's so quiet down here. The air is close and stale.

I step through the vault door and into the corridor beyond. The lights fade on, and my heart stops.

The doors are open. Eros's door is open wide, its shadow multiplied under the lights. Orpheus's door hangs only slightly ajar. But the corridor is empty.

There's no sign of them. Did they . . . did they go somewhere together?

I stand there frozen, unsure what to do. Part of me wants to run back the way I came, slam the vault door behind me and lock it, never to return. These open doors, the silence, everything bathed in a fluorescent glow . . . it gnaws at my nerves like a toothache. But I can't just run away like I'm *scared*. What do I think is going to happen? And I came all the way down here.

But Eros's words ring unwanted in my ears. *Don't trust him.*

'Shut up,' I mutter. 'Don't be a pussy, Katherine.'

The time it takes me to reach Eros's room feels like an eternity. At first, everything is completely quiet. It's like Ian came down here, opened the doors, and then left. But why? Was he in a drunken haze? Did he want to free his creations? Did he feel so guilty about calling Eros a whore that he decided to unleash him and Orpheus into the world, allowing them to live out some semblance of humanity? Yeah, as if.

As I move closer, I begin to hear a quiet sound. A soft, incessant buzz.

Someone, or some*thing*, is still here.

I walk slowly to the door and look in.

Ian isn't there. But Eros is.

Eros is all over the room. Scattered, fractured. Torn, limb from limb. Cut up and strewn. His legs are folded over one another on the far side of the room. One ankle is slashed, with wires sticking out at odd angles. One arm is on the dais, hand draped over the edge. The other arm lies a few feet away, broken in two places. His hand is in the far corner, opposite his legs. His torso lies at the foot of the dais, toga still wrapped around it, stained with electrical fluids. Wires and bits of machinery are everywhere.

His head is at my feet.

He stares up at me for a moment. Then his eyes roll back until all I can see are the whites. He blinks and his eyes roll down again, his blue gaze finding me. Fluid drips from his severed neck. It drips from his ears. The liquid is clear and thick as semen. I realize the buzzing sound is coming from Eros: some displaced wire, some gear half broken. I don't fucking know.

I brace myself on the door frame. I think I should speak. I should say something. I open my mouth, but nothing comes out.

Eros speaks for me. 'K-Katherine.' His voice is out of focus, warped like an old record. 'Fox. Fox. Katherine.'

'Kit.' I kneel then, placing my hands gently on either side of his face, holding him so he can look up at me. It feels like there's something caught in my throat, and I can't swallow it down. 'It's Kit, remember?'

Half of his mouth curves up in a smile. The buzzing stops, then starts again. 'Kit. Hello. H-hell . . . o Kit. Kit. Fox.'

'Who did this to you?' I whisper. My fingers shake as they brush a lock of flaxen hair from his forehead. 'Ian?' Ian, hating his own creation so much that he lost his mind? Ian, on a sexbot murder spree, fleeing his home and leaving me here to pick up the literal pieces?

Eros's eyes roll back. 'K-Kit.' His eyelids close, then open. 'Kit. I'm sorry.'

'Eros.' I stroke his temple with a thumb. 'It's okay. It's okay.'

His mouth twitches, and I can't tell if it's a smile or a grimace.

'Eros, please. Can you tell me what happened?'

'K-K-Kit.' Fluid from his ear drips down to my wrist, warm and thick. 'I'm sorry.'

'You did nothing wrong.'

His eyes roll back. 'K-Kit. Fo-o-ooox.'

The buzzing stops.

With violently shaking hands, I set Eros's head gently on the white floor. I grind my teeth together so hard my jaw pops. Someone ripped him apart. Someone destroyed him, tore him apart like he was nothing. And they made sure he was *awake* before it happened.

Not *someone*. Ian.

From far away, some logical, rational part of my brain shouts at me: *Eros is not a human. He's not sentient. He didn't understand what was happening.*

But the look in his eyes just now, the sorrow, the fact that he was apologizing . . . I bend over and vomit, the burn of whiskey and coffee and the remnants of my breakfast splattering on the white floor. Eros didn't feel like a robot. He felt like a person.

And what makes a person? I remember Ian's words from two nights ago: *Intellect. Emotion. Curiosity.* Eros had all of those. So what the fuck does Ian know about humanity?

I straighten, taking a deep breath. I push the hair out of my face and tuck it behind my ears. I don't look back at Eros when I leave the room. I don't want to remember him that way. Because as far as I'm concerned, the mechanical remnants all over the room are not him.

I think of Eros at the window, watching the rain. I think of his sweet smile, the way he spoke to me like I was the only person in the world. I think of the way he kissed me. His open smile. In my memory, he'll shine golden forever, like a summer sun.

# 14

Something desperate buzzes in my veins, a crackling need to fix this, even though I know I never could. Eros can't be glued back together again. He's as intricately made as a living thing, his filaments like twining DNA; the electric signals in his brain just as powerful and complex as a biological mind.

Whatever wonders he had to share with the world, whatever beauty or poetry or mind-blowing sex, is gone forever.

I stand in the corridor, hand braced on the wall, and remind myself that this isn't the only Eros. There are hundreds, maybe even thousands of models just like him in factories and private homes. He lives on, somewhere else. Some other Eros is looking out over a sun-drenched city right now, golden hair falling about his ears. He will never change. He will always be sweet and alluring.

Even knowing this, I can't stop shaking. My eyes burn with unshed tears. My mind can't convince my body that this is destruction of property, not a grisly murder. All I can think about is that Eros was like his child. Ian killed his own child.

And if a man can do that, then he's capable of anything.

Closing Eros's door behind me, I take a long, shaking breath. I don't have the energy to cry. I can do it later, once my knees are steady. Once my heart is no longer trying to climb up my throat and choke me.

Orpheus's room waits across the corridor.

I struggle to draw a full breath.

I'm terrified of what I'll feel when I see him ripped apart like Eros. I'm afraid it will drive me past some internal wall, and I'll tumble headfirst into the abyss that tempts me. That I'll lose something I never knew I'd miss until the moment I lost it. That I'll break irrevocably. Over a goddamn Pleasurebot.

I don't *need* to look, I tell myself. I don't need to see what Ian has done to Orpheus. I can just walk past the door and out of the vault, back upstairs. I can pack up my stuff and go. I never have to think about this god-forsaken place again.

But I know I won't.

I hold my breath outside the door. It's going to be okay. I'm going to be fine. It's just a robot. A computer program. A *thing*.

I pull the door all the way open and step through. The light fades on.

The room is empty.

My knees almost give out. He's not here. He's not dead. Not fucking *murdered*. But how? Why? A darker

136

thought flits across my mind: What if Ian took him somewhere? What if he's doing something even worse to Orpheus than what he did to Eros?

Sickness and relief war in me as I exit the vault. I leave the door as I found it, halfway open. By the time I get back upstairs, my lungs are burning, my heart thudding erratically. I feel hot, clammy, and dirty. I'm tainted by the thickly dripping fluids, sticky with the scent of mechanical death. I push open the door to the penthouse.

'Ian,' I say, hedging, just in case he's back.

There's no answer.

My chest is so tight. It's hard to breathe. I feel pulled to the window, suddenly desperate for its cool touch, for a semblance of fresh air, a glimpse of the world outside. I press a palm to the foggy glass, then touch the condensation to my hot forehead. I sigh as cool moisture soothes my aching head.

'Just chill out for a second,' I murmur. 'Then go. Pack your shit and go.'

I take a long breath in, a long breath out. I *will* be fine. Ian isn't dangerous. Not to *me*, I try to reassure myself, relaxing my eyes until the skyscrapers outside become dark blurs spotted with colorful light bursts. He's not going to hurt me. He's just drunk and frustrated with his Pleasurebot. He's just . . .

My thoughts judder to a halt.

Something is wrong. Something I can't place. It's

a tiny shock to the skin, a shallow splinter. I look out over the city. The skyline winks back at me through sheets of rain. The splinter of unease inches deeper. These buildings . . .

My stomach drops.

I don't recognize these buildings.

No, that can't be right. I rub at the glass where my breath has fogged. This window faces west. I know this view; I've been staring at it for two days. I *know* Los Angeles. I should be able to see the new cluster of mega-scrapers right there, glowing purple. I was admiring them this morning. I *remember*. And the half-abandoned business high-rise across the way, gold and blue-lit, always projecting neon ads, should be just there. But it isn't. Instead, the monoliths of black and neon are buildings I have never seen before, endless towering spires, violent and tooth-like silhouettes in the rain.

A sickening roil takes hold of my gut. The splinter drives deep into flesh, smarting, bleeding until I gasp at the disorientation. This isn't Los Angeles. I don't know any of these buildings. This is no city I'm familiar with.

A traffic drone whirrs past, half blinding me with its spinning red beams, and I reel back from the window.

I turn away from the glass expanse, desperate to anchor myself.

A dark figure stands in the kitchen, watching me.

A scream lodges in my throat. I freeze, every muscle

in my body going taut with fear, and then I recognize him.

'Fuck,' I spit the word like a rotten tooth dislodged. 'Orpheus, where the fuck did you *come from*?'

He drifts to me on long, elegant limbs. He moves like a figment of shadow or a dream. His silver hair catches the drone's light, glowing almost pink, a pulsing softness against my darkening fear.

'I'm here,' he says. His eyes are softly golden, his chest rising and falling. 'What's wrong?'

'I'm trapped in a fucking nightmare is what,' I gasp. Even in my heightened emotional state, I succumb to his gravity, allowing him to pull me gently into an embrace. His fingers drift through my hair. My cheek presses to his chest. 'Where were you? I tried to find you. Eros . . .' But the words catch in my throat. I can't say it. I don't want to make it real.

Orpheus strokes my back, my hair, murmuring exactly what I need to hear. 'You're afraid, Kit. Don't be afraid. I'm right here. I didn't go anywhere.'

The relief of his touch is a heady drug. Every word draws me in and softens me. I'm shaken apart by the molecule, laid out across the rain-dark sky until the world and I are one, and nothing can harm me. Every murmur of his voice paints calm across my nerves. He undoes me, little by little, until thoughts of Ian and Eros are far away. Until I'm utterly at Orpheus's mercy.

I tip my chin up to meet his eyes. It almost hurts to

look at him. He burns so brightly he's star-like. 'Thank God, you're alive. I went down to the vault, and you were gone, and I thought . . .'

He brushes my jaw with his knuckles. 'This body is not alive. It is a spectrum of electrical impulses and mechanical engineering.'

'I know. You're a computer, I know.'

'No, Kit. I am not.'

I pull away slightly, signals coming from far away, my brain shouting a distant warning. 'What?'

'This body is a machine,' he replies, leaning over me, his lips almost brushing mine. 'But I am not this body. I merely use it.'

This time, I pull away from him completely, palms against his chest, keeping him at arm's length. I look him up and down, his beautiful angles, broad shoulders, curving throat. My brain seems to be working impossibly slow. 'Say again?'

'I am not a computer. I am the mind that powers the machine.'

'Orpheus,' I say, suddenly unbelievably exhausted. 'What the fuck are you trying to say?'

'I told you I've been watching you,' he says. 'Do you know how? Do you understand why?'

'I thought it was . . . just a thing you tell girls.' I know it wasn't. I *know* what I felt with him last night, and what I feel now. Pure and undeniable connection, transcendent and soul-deep.

He chuckles, and I feel the low rumble in his chest in the palms of my hands. 'Kit, as far as I'm concerned, you are the only woman on Earth. No one else exists. You are *rare*. Do you not feel it? Have you not sensed it here in this house?'

My fingers curl in the soft fabric of his shirt. I'm standing at the edge of an impossible height, and I know I'm about to fall. 'Felt what?'

'Your gift.' He strokes my cheek with a knuckle. 'You must have felt it. The pull. There are a million worlds out there, Kit, waiting for you. You can step into any one of them. All you have to do is open the door.'

My body tenses. *Open the door.* I've heard that phrase before. Ian used it earlier. I thought he'd been on a drunken rant, prattling nonsense. 'Orpheus,' I say, dropping my hands and stepping away, putting even more distance between us. 'Please be straight with me for two seconds. I'm about to lose my goddamn mind, and nothing you or anyone else says in this fucking penthouse makes any sense.'

Something like hungry amusement flashes in Orpheus's gaze. 'Let me show you.'

'I don't know if that's . . .'

But he slides into my space like a quiet shadow and silences me with a kiss. Every thought in my head flies apart, blurring and fracturing. His mouth on mine is so exquisite, so heartbreaking in its intimacy, that I wonder how I ever lived without it. He touches me in ways I can't describe, delicate caresses combined with slow, firm movements against my body that drive me mad within seconds.

When he breaks the kiss, I try to drag his mouth back to mine, making a pathetic sound of frustration. But he stops me.

'Kit,' Orpheus says, gripping my head in his hands, his fingers buried in my hair. 'I'm going to need you to trust me. What you're about to experience will be unlike anything you've seen or felt before. But you need to see it. Are you ready?'

I don't know what I feel. I trust him. It's crazy, but I do. He is the embodiment of yearning, my daydreams given form. But I'm terrified of what he'll show me. How many fucked up things in my life are about to fall into place? 'I don't know.'

'There's no reason to be afraid. I won't force you. I'll follow every order you give me, as long as it brings you closer to rapture.'

*Fuck.* Those words alone light every synapse in my brain. Euphoria and desire flicker through me. I want him to devour me. 'Show me. I trust you.'

His eyes flare yellow. His hands find the small of my back and pull me in, and I'm already helpless in his grasp. 'Good. I want you to use me until there's nothing left. In this body, I exist only to bring you pleasure. And I want to give you the infinite universe.'

Orpheus kisses my neck, and everything fades to a

neon haze of pleasure. The penthouse is gone, and all that's left is sensation: Orpheus's mouth on my skin, his teeth dragging along my collarbone, his fingers in my hair. His hands all over me, pulling me in, in, in. I allow him to consume me like a black hole, atom by atom, my matter falling apart and re-forming even as he undoes me.

Time and movement are meaningless. Ecstasy drowns me in its undulation. It's like Orpheus was made for me and me alone; he knows where to touch, to stroke, to bite. He undresses me like a dance, as if every unbuttoning, every slide of fabric down my body, is an artist's expression. I can only cling to him, boneless, gasping, wet, and aching.

I'm naked when he finally enters me, his body unyielding at my back. He thrusts slowly as he palms my belly, as he caresses my peaked nipples, his teeth at my shoulder. My palms are pressed to the window. My breath is hot against the foggy glass.

He pushes deeper and I cry out, my cheek hitting the glass. My breasts flatten against the window. He rolls his hips, back pressed to mine as he thrusts into me over and over. Light-bright rain fills my vision until it blackens – I close my eyes, the world falls away – and the ache in my core tightens, tightens, tightens.

'You are different, Kit,' Orpheus murmurs, his low voice rumbling in my ear. I drift back to myself, shaking, teetering at the edge of orgasm. 'You're perfect. Unlike anyone else in this world.'

Orpheus thrusts in slowly, gently. His hand flattens against my belly. Then he pulls out, almost leaving me bereft. But as he does, he slides the fingers of his free hand between my legs, right where I need him most. 'I'm going to show you how perfect you are. Relax for me.'

I let out a shaking breath.

Then he slams his cock deep into me. At the same time, his fingers find a pressure that needs releasing. Everything tightens. The ache grows impossible. I whisper his name, pleading.

Just as I begin to fall over the edge, tears in my eyes, the feeling so full and so bright that it might kill me –

'There,' he says. 'Open your eyes. Look.'

I open my eyes.

The skyline flares in colored light as I come, blurred with tears and rain-smeared glass. He holds me as wave after wave of pleasure engulfs me. But even as I fall into that incomprehensible bliss, the city outside wavers. Each light sparks out, one by one, as if covered up by a shadowy hand.

At the crest of my orgasm, I gasp his name, *Orpheus*.

Then something catches my eye. The smallest thing, a glimmer in my periphery.

I glance down.

My body is – is glitching. Parts of it shimmer in and

out. It's fuzzy at the edges, like an old television, lines of static running through me. It's like the mirage from before, but it's *part* of me this time. I'm the mirage. I gasp in horror.

My entire body disappears, then reappears, flickering like a dying lightbulb.

Fuck, fuck, *fuck*.

Orpheus's hand between my thighs is still moving, still urging me on.

But my orgasm dies as terror and confusion win out, and I wrench myself from Orpheus's grasp. I fall to my knees at the window. That now-familiar pressure bears down on me, the intensity of being crushed beneath an impossible weight, like I'm miles underwater. My ears pop painfully.

'What the *fuck*,' I gasp, heaving for breath, not sure if I'm taking in too much oxygen or not enough. I hold up my hands, turning them front to back. They're whole and solid. I look down at my naked body, heaving and wet with perspiration. It's also whole and solid.

Orpheus holds out a hand.

I stare up at him. His eyes glow gold, his face unreadable. The city outside lights the planes of his face. His hair falls in pristine waves over one shoulder. He shows no sign of fear, confusion, or exertion.

'What the fuck just happened?' My voice is weaker the second time, lost and afraid. I wrap my arms around myself. I'm humiliated by my nakedness, my tears, my fear.

Orpheus kneels before me, cupping my face in his hands. 'It was a door to another world,' he says softly, almost wondering, almost worshiping. 'You opened it, and you looked through.'

# 15

I try to catch my breath, but panic overrides my body. I hiccup, choking on tears. The sight of my body like that, blurred and insubstantial, burns in my mind. The darkness spreading over the city. The heavy weight of it all, the crush against my bones. 'A *door*?' I echo, incredulous. 'No. *No*. My body was disappearing. Flickering. I was blinking out of fucking existence. What the hell do you mean, a door?'

Orpheus tucks a strand of sweat-matted hair behind my ears. 'You might describe it more accurately as a bridge.'

'A *what*?'

His gaze softens. 'A bridge between worlds. *Our* worlds, more specifically. You reach out, sometimes, when you sleep. When your consciousness is untethered to reality. And when you do, you glow like a beacon. Did you know that? I could see you from worlds away.'

I stare up at him from where I'm sprawled naked on the floor, my breaths coming in short, sharp bursts. It takes me a moment to register his words, and another to understand them. But it doesn't make sense. If he's saying what I think he is, then . . .

But it doesn't make *sense*.

I glance around until I see my discarded sweater, my skirt, and there – still folded, half fallen out of my skirt pocket – the paper from Ian's study. I lean sideways and pluck the paper from the carpet. Time seems to slow as I unfold it. Smoothing its creases, I stare down at the page laid out on the ground before me. The sketch of that strange, jagged shape. The mirage.

*A door to another world.*

'This is a . . .' the word catches in my throat. 'A wormhole? The door you're talking about. It's this?' I hold up the paper.

What the ever-loving fuck? That mirage was a crack in space-time, or a wormhole, or a kind of portal?

'Call it what you like,' says Orpheus, reaching for me. 'Ian calls it a door.'

I'm dumbstruck. A million different thoughts blaze through my head.

Orpheus hooks his hands under my arms and lifts me effortlessly, cradling me against him. He moves us to the couch and sits, gathering me in his lap with my back to his chest, facing away from the window. Pulling a throw blanket over us, he covers my nakedness. He strokes my hair. Runs a soft hand down my arm.

'I don't get it,' I whisper after a few minutes of quiet.

'I told you, I am not this body,' Orpheus says, voice

thick with affection. 'I only inhabit it. I am not from your world. I came here through a door like the one you just opened. And I know that you are gifted, because I've been watching you from my world.'

'How is that possible?'

He exhales slowly. 'My people perceive things that others can't. We drift close to the veils between worlds, sensing what's beyond. But this ability is *nothing* compared to yours. Your power burns as brightly as a star. Ever since I first saw you, I knew you were one of the few who can naturally do what others spend years, lifetimes, trying to achieve: You can open doors.'

Everything feels dull. Far away. Even Orpheus's voice fades as he speaks, turning to static as my mind rejects what he's saying. It's impossible. It's ridiculous. Science fiction. I don't care what I post on my blog about multiverse theory, I know it's not *real*.

My breath catches as a memory comes to me. Ian talking over breakfast, going on and on about this building. How he built it on a geomagnetic hot spot, a convergence of ley lines, energetic paths across the world that enhance psychic power, magic, all the shit I blog about.

Everything was fine until I came *here*. It's the penthouse, these ley lines. The shadowy figures, the vertigo, even the city changing. Everything I thought were hallucinations were really shadows from another world, my ability trying to manifest.

'I really hate all of this,' I say. 'Why me? And why does it hurt?'

Orpheus kisses the top of my head, wrapping his arms around me. 'It hurts because it's new to you. Like a child taking her first steps. You're bound to fall.'

I chew the inside of my mouth. There are still so many questions buzzing in my head, but at least my fear is dissipating. 'But that paper I found in the study,' I object. 'That drawing of a wormhole and my name. Ian knew somehow. He knew about my gift. How?' I spin on Orpheus, suddenly realizing, pulling away. A piece of the puzzle falls into place. 'You're the mind that controls the machine. Ian made the machine. Ian *brought* you here.'

'Yes.' Orpheus watches me with an openness that unsettles me. There's nothing wary in his gaze, no hidden truth.

'So you told him about me; you got him to hire me for some reason?' A pang of realization. 'Jesus, is the book even real?'

'I did not tell Ian about your gift,' Orpheus says, reaching for me.

I edge further away on the couch. My heart twists in grief, betrayal. 'I don't think I believe you.'

'You have to trust me.'

'I don't trust anyone in this penthouse. Not you, not Ian.'

I have no idea what time it is; darkness stretches endlessly over the city. Rain pounds on the window.

I wonder if the rain will ever let up. Or if it will keep coming, drumming on the ceiling, the streets, the Hollywood Hills, until everything flows into the ocean, washed clean.

Dread coils in my stomach as I remember the alien spires of an unknown city. I turn to the window, holding my breath, expecting the worst. But there are the familiar mega-scrapers. The cellphone ads. The Los Angeles skyline. Home.

I turn back to meet Orpheus's gaze. His eyes are still pools of honey, unreadable.

'And Eros?' Orpheus murmurs. 'Do you trust him?'

A swoop of nausea in my gut. 'He's dead. Destroyed. I found him in the vault, violently torn apart.'

Orpheus's expression doesn't change. 'I know you were fond of Eros. Ian is known to have a temper. He was never satisfied with that model.'

I shake my head, biting the inside of my cheek. My eyes burn. The traitorous choke of tears threatens at the base of my throat. I don't want to cry; I don't want to be vulnerable. Not now, when all that's between me and Orpheus is a thin blanket and a few feet of space. Not now, when my world is falling apart.

'You needn't mourn him,' Orpheus says, reaching for my hand and taking it in his. His thumb swipes delicate circles over my skin. 'He and I are not the same. He was a program. He was engineered.'

I remember the way Eros's face sometimes changed,

the way he seemed like he wanted to say something but couldn't. His warning still rings in my ears. But I don't have the energy to argue with Orpheus. I don't have the energy for anything. He's probably right; Eros was, and is, nothing but a robot. Everything that seemed human about him was designed that way. And everything else was my own mind playing tricks on me.

'Come here,' Orpheus murmurs, grasping my hand and pulling me toward him, my back against his chest, into his embrace. I don't resist. I let him envelop me. Because even now, he feels familiar. He feels like comfort. He feels like home. He wraps me in his arms, and I let out a long, shaking breath.

'This should have been an easy job,' I breathe. 'An interview, a book, a career. But just like everything else I touch, it's fucking falling apart. Ruined.'

He rests his chin on the top of my head, and I can't help but melt against him. 'Kit,' he says, 'you are pure. An innocent soul, luminous and sweet. There is nothing you could ruin that is not already rotten.'

I feel myself pulled into him, unable to resist. But I'm afraid that if I kiss him, I'll never stop. I'll let him kiss me until I stop caring about the world around me, until I'm starved, until I fade away into nothing.

'I need to talk to Ian,' I say, restless, needing to be distracted.

Orpheus's hands rove under the blanket and over my still-naked body.

My heart staccatos, my skin too sensitive. I feel like I'm in a liminal space, suspended between reality and dream. I gasp as Orpheus's hand slides over my breast. And God, I hate that he feels so good, so right.

But I have so many questions.

'Why did Ian . . .' I start, but Orpheus's fingers move lower to the sensitive skin below my ribs, and my brain shorts out.

He pushes my hair out of the way, kissing my neck. His other hand seeks lower. 'Do you want to speak of Ian right now?'

A wave of want engulfs me. 'No, but . . . *ah, fuck*. I want . . . I need . . .'

He grabs one thigh with a strong hand, pulling my legs apart. 'What do you want, Kit? What do you need?'

I make a humiliating sound, a pleading gasp at the back of my throat. 'Do not speak of Ian when I am inside you,' Orpheus says softly. Then he eases a finger into me, where I'm tight and wet and desperate. He moves the finger in and out, pumping slowly.

'*God,* Orpheus,' I breathe. 'But –'

Another finger joins the first, and my hips buck without my permission. 'But what?'

My brain utterly gives up then, fluttering limply into hedonism as I ride his fingers.

Orpheus rumbles approval at the base of my ear, his lips brushing my skin. 'Mine is the only name you will speak when you're like this.'

Then he bites down on my neck, just hard enough to smart, at the same time sliding a third finger inside me. I choke on a cry of pleasure, reaching back with one hand to grab his hair, mindless and writhing in his lap. The growing pressure of his fingers inside me is too much; his mouth on my skin is too much. Everywhere he touches skitters bright with sparks of desire.

Then he finally gives me what I need, pressing the heel of his hand to my aching core.

'Come for me,' he says. 'Tell me I'm yours.'

It's all too easy to obey.

*You are mine. Mine. Mine.*

Orpheus makes no effort to achieve his own release. He holds me until I lie still, breathing hard, both appeased and unbelievably frustrated. And beneath it all, beneath the drug of Orpheus that hangs heavy over my mind and body, I remember that he is not a human. He is not a Pleasurebot.

He's something else. Something altogether unknowable.

It's late in the evening, and Ian still hasn't come home. Orpheus and I have fucked, made love, had sex – every iteration of the act – so many times that I've lost count. He's insatiable, unstoppable, and never fails to wring an incredible orgasm out of me. I let him because I need it. I need this, the closeness, the ecstasy, the distraction. And I'll ride Orpheus's cock as many times as it takes for me to return to some semblance of sanity.

I roll over in bed, where our latest fuck has taken us. It's rainy, dark, and intimate here. Orpheus's naked body, smoothed at the edges by darkness, glows pale in the city lights. His hair falls over his shoulders, unmussed by hours of sex.

I should try to rest. I should let the soporific effects of Orpheus's cock lull me to sleep so I might wake up refreshed in the morning. I should worry about Ian in the morning. I should worry about *me* in the morning. But the billionaire's absence and Eros's subsequent death scratch at the inside of my brain until I can't take it anymore.

'I'm worried about Ian,' I admit. 'He didn't leave a note. I don't get it. I don't understand what he wants from me. Obviously not a book.' Bitterness drips from my tongue. I can't help it; I'm fucking pissed. This book was supposed to change my life. Instead, I'm grappling with unthinkable truths about myself and the universe, wondering what Ian De Leon could possibly want with me.

'Don't worry about him,' Orpheus says acidly. 'He would never extend the same courtesy to you.'

I look for meaning in Orpheus's expression. 'Tell me why.'

Orpheus shifts behind me, pulling me to him until my back is pressed to his chest. As he speaks, he nuzzles my neck with his nose. 'Because Ian's ego overshadows his sense. He's blessed with intellect but never uses it for good. He could feed the starving. He could fund your planet's colonization effort. If he wanted to, he could plant a million forests, revolutionize solar energy, and turn back the clock on this dying world. Instead, he builds caricatures of love. He seeks to open doors that are not his to access. He brought me here against my will. He lied to you, and with that deceitful mouth, he dared to taste you.'

I blow out a shaking breath. 'I just don't understand why he did that to Eros. His first working model. Gone. He seemed so proud of him at first.'

'Ian does not love what he creates,' Orpheus says, more gently than before. 'He wants to rule over it. That's all.'

'Okay, well. I just . . .' A knot lodges in my throat. The book isn't real. Eros is dead. Ian is missing. My life has changed, but not in the way I needed it to. Everything about this whole experience has been nothing but a nightmare I want to forget. Everything but Orpheus. I close my eyes tight, willing the tears away.

'Kit,' Orpheus breathes. He strokes my hair, pulling me tightly to him. He mouths along the length of my neck, his fingers tracing circles on my stomach. As always, his touch is calming, his voice a drug. 'Don't cry. Whatever Ian has done to Eros is not your concern. Humans are messy, contradictory creatures.'

'But —'

'Shh,' he soothes, pressing kisses to my temple. 'Ian suffers great turmoil. But you don't need to suffer. Let me kiss you. Let me undo you. Let me quell your pain with untold pleasure.'

He touches me slowly, deliberately. He croons incandescent words in my ear, calling me beautiful, perfect, breathtaking.

'I've been waiting so long to meet you,' he says. 'I missed you. I'd never met you, but I missed you.'

I relax into him as he strokes me from collarbone to belly, softly pulling at my thighs with long fingers, opening my legs. 'Let me show you all the pleasure a human body can sustain, and then I'll give you more.'

I arch back against him, already wet and needy. God, despite everything, I want this. I *need* it. The way his hands play over my skin is supernatural. My thoughts short out as he enters me from behind, and I sink into his orbit, riding waves of bliss until I forget the world entirely.

All that exists is Orpheus, a live electrical current crackling in the darkness, and I throw myself into him, unflinching.

'How many lovers have made you feel this way?' He thrusts slowly as he asks, his fingers digging into the flesh of my hips. His breath is hot on my ear.

'None,' I gasp, turning my head to face him.

He kisses me from that awkward angle, needy and breathless. My mind flickers in a near-unconscious state as I surface from the agonizing pleasure. My body tightens in an overwhelming ache as I come, riding wave after wave of perfect rapture.

*Orpheus*, I think I cry his name.

'How many have brought you to climax like this, better than you thought was possible?'

I come undone against him, my breath coming in small gasps. He is solid behind me, holding me steady, a gorgeous anchor to keep me from falling forever. I think of all those nights I've spent with men – some I thought I loved, most I hardly knew. Their fumbling fingers, their messy kisses. The sex I thought would make me whole and the cold emptiness that followed.

Orpheus leans over me, pressing his lips to my temple. His silver-bright hair tickles my sensitive skin. Every muscle in my body is lax. My thoughts come slowly, trapped in syrupy bliss.

'None,' I answer. 'You're the only one.'

He smiles against me, face nestled in the crook of my neck and shoulder. His cock is still inside me, his fingers trailing delicate lines down my belly. Already, the flame of need blooms again inside me like a lit match.

'Good,' Orpheus murmurs. 'Good. You'll need no one else after me.'

# 16

I wake to the sound of the wind. It shrieks at the windows, and rain skitters sideways across the glass. It's freezing in my room. I sit up in the dark, lit only by the city lights outside. I'm alone in my bed. What time is it? Memories from last night rush to the forefront: Orpheus inside me, all around me, touching me, speaking to me softly until I was limp and pliant.

Ian, missing.

Eros, violently exterminated.

The vision of Eros's broken body grips me, and I throw my arms over my eyes, groaning. God, if only it could all be nothing but a fucked up dream. Orpheus is gone, but I know from the soreness between my legs, the dried sweat on my skin, that last night was all too real. And lying here feeling sorry for myself won't change anything.

Still naked, I roll out of bed and go to the bathroom. I run the tap and splash cold water on my face, relishing the soothing chill.

'Don't be a pussy, Katherine,' I say, but it's barely more than a whisper.

Lifting my head to face the mirror, I'm greeted with the reflection of a girl I'm not sure I know anymore. Nothing about my outward appearance has changed. My hair is a mess, sleep-mussed and tangled with sex. But instead of a fringe science blogger with a penchant for bad choices, I see a girl who has witnessed things she'll never forget. Things she wishes she could scrape from her brain like cancerous tissue.

I pull my hair into a bun, tucking stray strands behind my ears. Then I lock eyes with myself in the mirror. 'I'm leaving,' I say aloud. And I mean it.

But what about Orpheus? My heart betrays me, making me hesitate.

I turn away from the mirror. Grabbing whatever clothes are at the top of my duffle, I get dressed breathlessly. Then I pack up my toiletries, shove them in the duffle, zip it shut, and heft it onto my shoulder. Forget Orpheus. I'm getting out of here, and that's that. I'm never coming back to this house of horrors that sways among the storm clouds. I'm going back to a world that makes sense. A life that makes sense, a Katherine Fox who makes sense.

But my heart is already beginning to fracture at the thought of never seeing Orpheus again.

I jog down the spiral staircase. Unsurprisingly, the penthouse is empty. These assholes keep disappearing on me. Afraid that if I stop moving, I'll change my mind, I go straight to the hall closet and yank on my trench, then my boots, lacing them up messily. My hands are shaking. The wind doesn't relent. It howls and howls until the building itself sounds like it's about to fly apart in the gale.

When I'm fully dressed, duffle in hand, I speed walk across the living area, pointedly not looking out the window. I'm still utterly alone. A knot settles in my throat as I stop before the elevator.

A strong gust of wind drives freezing rain against the window, startling me. But I still refuse to look. No, just go, I tell myself. I exhale slowly, counting down from ten in a sad attempt to soothe my anxiety. No matter what lies beyond that rain-blurred window, what buildings break the clouds and watch like blackened teeth, they won't exist outside this place. They can't.

I press the button to call the elevator.

The wind lets up for a moment as I wait. The rain stops pounding against the glass. And in that breath of quiet, I hear it: a distant moan. A cry of pain or fear.

My heart stops.

Then the wind picks up, and the sound is gone, washed away by the shrieking gale and the drum of rain.

The elevator dings. The door slides open, inviting me in.

*Come on, let's go,* the empty elevator seems to say. *Forget all of this.*

And God, I want to.

But my traitor feet are planted to the ground. Because that pained sound is echoing in my head, curdling my stomach.

'Get in the elevator, Katherine.' But my voice is weak.

I put a hand inside the elevator doors, holding them open with light pressure. But I don't step in.

*Get in the fucking elevator.*

No. I can't. Because suddenly, I have this horrible, sickening feeling that Ian is here, back in the vault. That he's going to tear Orpheus apart, just like Eros. Finally putting an end to the disobedient mistake.

The duffle falls from my fingers and clatters to the floor. I'm already halfway to the door to the vault when the elevator doors slide shut behind me. I key in the door code with trembling fingers, wrenching the door open the second it unlocks.

I fly down the stairs. Barely thinking, barely *breathing*.

Another hoarse, pained cry cuts through the silence, the only other sounds my heartbeat and frantic foot-steps on the stairs.

I miss the last step on the flight and skid, landing painfully on my tailbone. I hiss in pain, but I keep going.

It sounds like Ian is torturing Orpheus down there. He might be cutting him apart right now, wrench-ing his limbs from his body with a horrible strength, driven by madness or rage. I don't know what I'll do when I get there. But the thought of Orpheus's perfect body, his face so beautiful it could be holy, being ripped apart nearly drives me insane.

The vault door is still open.

I rush through it, heart pounding, my lungs aflame. My back throbs where I fell, but I'm here now.

I'll save him. I have to.

The doors are open, just like before. I stop at Eros's room and glance in, seeing only the remains of his beautiful mechanical body. I grit my teeth. There's only one room left. The door stands open.

A strangled groan pierces the silence. It's clearer now, and distinctly human in its agony.

Adrenaline spikes through me as I cross to the door. It has to be Orpheus, dying. Orpheus, his eyes darkening. No, no, *no*, not like this. Not before I have a chance to —

Just inside the doorway, I freeze.

Confusion grips me, and I stare dumbly at the scene before me.

Ian sits with his back against the far wall, slumped, his legs stretched out before him. He's breathing heavily, taking shallow, labored breaths. Usually so well-groomed and pristine, he is strikingly disheveled. Black curls hang over a pallid forehead. His shirt is wrinkled and hanging open, the collar rumpled. His sickly face is a mess of sweat. His eyes are bloodshot. Blood drips thickly from one of his nostrils, staining his shirt.

Belatedly, the smell hits me, acrid and metallic: sweat, and the sickly tang of fear.

He seems to notice me slowly, lifting his head just enough to peer at me through half-shut eyes. 'Kit?'

'Ian.' I inch closer, unsure of exactly what I'm seeing. I have even less of an idea of what to say. When I'm close enough that his smell nearly gags me, I stop. I think he might have pissed himself. His eyes have closed again; he's breathing slowly but steadily.

'Ian,' I say again. But my voice is weak, unsteady, and breaks as I speak. 'What the hell happened?'

His eyes flutter open. 'Kit,' he croaks. 'Help me.'

The wind howls a distant song all around us.

I stay exactly where I am. I'm not doing anything until I understand what the fuck is going on. 'What *happened*, Ian?'

But he only laughs, a broken, mad chuckle.

'*Ian*,' I snap, hearing my voice as though from far away.

'Either help me,' he says, his head lolling so as to look at me head-on. He holds my gaze through wet lashes, with sweat or tears, I can't tell. 'Or fucking *leave*.'

Every instinct in me screams to obey. Ian is clearly in pain, delirious. 'What do you need? An ambulance?'

He groans, closing his eyes. 'No, no . . . I fucked up, Kit. I fucked up.'

I grit my teeth. Fine. If he's not going to tell me anything, then I should go. Whatever happened to Ian is

Ian's goddamn problem now. It's more than likely that he came home blackout drunk, wandered down here, passed out, and pissed himself.

But something in his eyes makes me stay. Something darker, something sharp-edged. 'Where's Orpheus?'

Ian laughs, another harrowing, unhinged bark. 'Where's *Orpheus*? Fucking Christ. He has you twisted around his finger, and you don't even . . .' He lets his head fall back against the wall as he trails off, eyes still closed. 'Forget it. Fuck off and leave me here.'

My throat tightens. 'What the fuck are you talking about?'

'Or you can stick around,' Ian mutters. 'Find out.'

I've had enough of his self-absorbed bullshit. I kneel at his side, grabbing his shoulders roughly with my hands, and shake him. His eyes fly open, red-rimmed. 'Tell me what's going *on*, Ian. Now!'

He coughs, a spluttering, laughing exhalation. 'Nothing, Kit. Nothing's going on. All I did was follow orders.'

'What the fuck does *that* mean?'

A sound, soft, almost imperceptible, catches my ear.

I look back. And there he is, shadowed in the doorway, draped in black with shining golden eyes: Orpheus.

# 17

Filaments of unseen electricity seem to spark between the three of us. I clench my hands into tight fists, as if I can hold onto the fabric of the world I understand and not lose it forever.

Ian laughs again. It's a sickening, hateful sound. 'Orpheus, Orpheus. See? Even *you* make mistakes. Should've killed me faster. Now she knows.' Ian's gaze flits hazily to me. 'He thinks he's better than us.'

I glare at Ian. 'I already know about Orpheus,' I spit. 'He told me where he came from. I know the book was never real. And I *know* what you did to Eros, you murdering piece of shit.'

Ian makes a choked sound that might be another laugh, but it turns into a violent cough, blood spattering his lips. 'You can't murder a machine.'

'He was more than that,' I say, my words low and heavy with anger. 'Eros was so much more than a machine. But you're never satisfied, are you? You what, opened a door? Dragged Orpheus into our world and shoved him into a Pleasurebot? And then you destroyed your own creation because he couldn't participate in your . . . your fucking faux intellectual conversations?'

'Don't make me laugh,' Ian says. 'Orpheus is –'

'What she says is true,' Orpheus cuts him off, taking two more steps forward, his gaze crackling with heat. 'I was made a prisoner in this body.'

'Dramatic,' Ian snipes. 'Always so dramatic. I promised you everything you wanted, and you rejected it. She's here, isn't she? But you betrayed me. So end it, already. I don't fucking care. Get it over with.'

'Wait, what's that supposed to mean?' I snap. Acid roils in my gut. *She's here, isn't she?* Silence drags on for several seconds as Ian and Orpheus stare hatred at one another. 'Hello? One of you assholes care to enlighten me?'

Ian looks at me, our faces almost level, and for a moment, the animosity drains from his face. All that's left is sadness. Loneliness. And I wonder for a second if this is the real Ian, raw and afraid, in over his head. But then he sneers, and his expression closes, and his face becomes a cold mask of indifference. 'You were supposed to be his little present.'

I look up at Orpheus. But his expression is unreadable; his attention is focused on Ian. I turn back to Ian, feeling sick. I remember the paper, the drawing of the mirage, my name . . . and those four words: *He insists on her*.

'I could have brought in any girl in LA,' Ian continues.

'There are hundreds of thousands to choose from. But Orpheus wanted *you*.'

'Leave her out of this,' Orpheus rumbles.

'You're the one who brought her into it,' Ian growls. 'What did you expect would happen when you made your demands? It's not my fault you chickened out.'

Orpheus looms above us like a storm cloud, and I can't help but shrink away at the sight. His face is a mask of calm hatred, cold-edged and as distant as the moon. His lip curls. 'You're a fool to think I would honor your bargain, Ian De Leon. You are weak. You are *nothing*.'

The wind howls. Whatever grip I thought I had on my world is lost forever, and I'm scrambling desperately to keep up.

'Tell me what the fuck bargain you made,' I say to the room at large, 'or I'll fucking drag you both up to the roof and throw you off it.' It's an empty threat, but in that moment, heart pounding and adrenaline screaming through my veins, I almost believe I could do it.

Ian turns to me, eyes blazing. 'Whatever Orpheus told you, don't believe it. He came here, and he was fucking insatiable. Insatiable.'

I glance at Orpheus, but he remains silent, his lips a tight line, his eyes blazing.

'Okay, and?' I demand, looking expectantly between them both. *Insatiable?* My mind latches on to the word, seeking a lifeline to logical meaning. 'What are you trying to tell me, that Orpheus is a sex-crazed being from another dimension? That when he said he saw me from worlds away and wanted to fuck me, you . . . what, hired me to write your fake biography? So you could indulge his fantasy?' The explanation sounds fucking ridiculous, but it's the only one I can come up with.

'Kit,' Orpheus cuts in, his voice low, a warning.

I spin on him. 'Well?'

'Oh, put a sock in it, bitch,' Ian says, his voice growing audibly weaker despite the venom in his words. His voice pitches higher as he speaks, a whine of despair. 'It doesn't matter. It's all fucked now. It's all fucked.'

'Speak to her like that again,' Orpheus says in a glassy tone, 'and I will make sure you die slowly and in unspeakable agony. You are nothing to her. She is above you, better than you, beyond you in every possible way. She accomplishes with ease what you spent years of your pathetic life trying to do. And yet, you treat her like she's nothing. You kissed her like she was nothing. You *touched* her like she was no one. And now, you give her orders, you insult her, and with every breath, you step closer to the edge of a bottomless abyss.'

As he speaks, Orpheus seems to grow taller, more imposing, more terrifying. Shadows gather behind him, his eyes glowing like twin suns. His hair lifts in an unseen wind, and for a moment, he looks just like a dark god, come down to punish us lesser beings.

'Do it, then,' Ian barks. More blood comes up and colors his lips. 'If I'm such a worm, then end this. Finish what you started.'

'No one is finishing anything until you assholes stop arguing and tell me,' I turn to Orpheus, '*clearly*, what role I'm serving in this Shakespearean drama.'

Orpheus remains silent as a statue, making my blood boil. I spin on Ian. '*Well?*'

Ian swallows, half-choking on what I can only imagine is his own blood, and sighs. 'Fine. You want to know what I did? I opened an interdimensional door.' His tone is deadpan, the voice of a man facing death with resigned certainty. 'I bridged an impossible gap between worlds. I accessed a place that should never have been fucking accessed. I spent years working just to get a glimpse of it. It was *supposed* to be beautiful. I thought the beings who lived there would be beautiful, too. I *needed* them to be. They would solve the puzzle of my Eros. Ignorant, stupid Eros. I thought if I opened this door . . . I thought I could invite something else in. A soul to live in my creations. A mind to fill the body.'

'What the fuck,' I say, withering, 'does that have to do with me?'

Ian suddenly comes to life, reaching for me, his fingers opening and closing around thin air. His mouth twists in disgust. 'I tried to send him back. But the door wouldn't open again, Kit. It wouldn't open. I tried to keep him fed. I tried. But people were starting to notice. The disappearances . . . I had to stop him. I'm not the monster. *He* is. He threatened me . . .' Ian pauses, his breathing harsh and laborious. 'He said he'd . . . he'd fucking eat *me* if I didn't give him what he wanted.'

Blood roars in my ears, and I get slowly to my feet. 'Eat you,' I repeat. Sweat dots my upper lip. I turn slowly. Orpheus stands utterly still, watching me with those golden eyes. I can still feel his hands on me, tender and reverent. The Orpheus I know and the one Ian is describing are two different beings entirely. They have to be. 'Orpheus? Were you going to *eat* Ian?'

'Yes.'

The floor falls out from under me. 'You eat . . . people.'

'I consume life,' he says. 'Vivacity. Souls.'

I try to keep my composure, even as time seems to screech to a halt. I move away from Ian, unsteady on my feet. Orpheus still looms between me and the doorway, a long lost lover; a complete and total stranger.

My instincts tell me to run. But I know my traitorous feet would take me straight into his fucking arms. I don't trust anyone in this room, least of all myself.

'Let me go,' I say, hoarse and unsteady. 'I won't say a word about any of this. I'm under NDA. I won't say a fucking thing; I swear to God.'

Orpheus's expression softens, gazing at me with an impenetrable sadness. He moves toward me, one hand lifted as if he wants to reach for me but holds back. 'I was never going to hurt you, Kit. I couldn't.'

I back away, my heart slamming an endless warning against my ribs. 'I don't believe you.' I turn sharply to Ian, spitting my words. 'You were going to *feed* me to Orpheus, so you made up a story to get me here. Isn't that *right*?' My voice breaks on the question.

'You really are stupid if you thought I'd actually publish a book about myself,' Ian says weakly. He coughs, and the blood stands out bright on his pallid skin. His eyes are half-closed, his breath slow and shallow.

'You're vile,' I grind out through clenched teeth. I try to ride this flare of anger, knowing that if I allow myself to be truly, wholly afraid, I will crumble. And then something occurs to me. Three words, spoken by a sweet, sun-bright voice. I turn to Orpheus in what feels like slow motion. 'Eros warned me. He warned me not to trust you. I thought he meant Ian, but he was talking about *you*.'

Orpheus's eyes spark yellow. 'Yes, Kit. Eros saw me as a monster. So does Ian. But you don't have to.'

'Run,' says Ian. His voice is barely audible, his skin paper-white. 'Run, Kit. He doesn't care about you. He's a predator.' Then his gaze slips past me like he's speaking to someone else entirely. 'I'm sorry, Eros . . . God, I'm sorry . . . I'm sorry I let him in . . .' he trails off, his head slumping on his chest.

I back away from Orpheus until I hit the far wall. He stays motionless, only his gaze holding me from across the room. Orpheus couldn't have. He wouldn't, it's impossible. But Ian's words cut like a knife.

'Orpheus,' I say, my voice breaking. 'Did you destroy Eros?'

Orpheus says nothing. He remains exactly where he is, still as a statue. But I see it in his eyes.

A rush of horror grips me.

'Why?' I choke. 'Eros didn't *have* a soul.'

'He did,' Orpheus says quietly. 'You recognized in Eros what Ian was blind to. He was so much more than a machine. And if I hadn't fed on him, I would have lost control, and you would be dead.'

Hot tears sting my eyes. 'You're a fucking monster.'

'Congrats,' Ian says weakly from the floor, clearly with great effort. 'Took you long enough.'

A wave of inexorable rage crashes over me. Ian's face, the smug twist of his mouth, is so hateful that my skin itches with it. My blood boils. I remember the way he told me we were friends, equals, the way he gushed about my blog, the way he kissed me. It was all a lie. It was all a trap, and Eros is dead, and it's all Ian's fucking fault.

'Shut the *fuck* up, Ian.' I'm vibrating with fury, and I let the feeling overtake me. 'You invited me here to die. You knew I would go to Orpheus. You fucked me, knowing your interdimensional pet was going to *eat* me. You're beyond redemption, dickhead. Orpheus may be a monster, Ian, but monsters can be tamed. Your soul is rotten to the fucking core. And I don't think it's going to taste very good.'

Orpheus turns to me, his eyes darker than I've ever seen them. And I *hate* that I don't hate him, that I'm still drawn to him, monstrous as he is. That he feels like home.

'Well?' I prompt, jerking my head toward Ian. 'Finish him off.'

Orpheus suddenly rushes Ian, moving unbelievably fast, crouching over his body, his broad shoulders hunched. I turn away, heading for the door. I don't want to see whatever Orpheus does to a human; I don't want to think about what he did to Eros. I don't want to think about anything. Even though I'm sure I'll spend the rest of my life yearning for a voice, a touch, a soul I can't have, I have to leave him behind. I have to get the fuck out of here.

As I pass through the threshold into the corridor, I hear Ian grunt once, a low, hoarse sound. And then there is nothing but silence.

# 18

My pulse roars in my ears, adrenaline rushing in my veins. Too-bright light glares down as I grab the door. I move to slam it shut behind me, to lock Orpheus inside.

I almost make it.

The door is nearly shut when Orpheus's hand shoots through the gap, fingers clamping around the edge. His impossible strength wrenches the door open, and I stumble at the force of it. I never stood a chance.

He says he won't hurt me. But my instincts kick in, and I spin on my heel. I try to run.

But before I can take more than one step, Orpheus's arm snakes around my middle and jerks me backward, slamming me hard against his chest. I scream, kicking, trying to get away. But his strength is inhuman. And I know deep down, even as I wrestle against his hold on me, that this is it. I'll never leave this vault. I'll never see Los Angeles again. I'll never watch the sun set over the ocean. I'll never stand under the rain. Just like Eros and Ian, these concrete walls and fluorescent lights will be the last thing I ever see.

'Orpheus,' I beg, a last, weak attempt. 'Please let me go.'

'Stop,' he says, calm but firm. His breath ruffles my hair. 'I'm not going to hurt you.'

I don't think I believe that. I don't know. I *want* to believe it. I'm desperate, *dying* to believe it.

I realize there's no point in struggling. I fall still, breathing hard.

'*Kit.*'

He speaks my name like a resonant spell. And as that single syllable sears me, he takes hold of my jaw from behind, forcing me to still.

I close my eyes tight, waiting for whatever comes next. Will he break my neck? Will he devour me?

My vision wavers. And it comes to me. The obvious, the glaring elephant in the room. Can I do it? Can I grasp the filamental threads of an unseen, impossible power, and stitch together an escape out of pure stubborn desperation?

I have to try.

Orpheus says something, his breath hot on my ear. But I'm not listening.

Because I'm focused on the air in front of me. I'm remembering how it felt every time the world fell out from under me, when my body glitched and flickered in the darkness, when the mirage opened up before me. I'm remembering the sensation, the sound, how my skin seemed to tighten, my body crushed under the pressure. I reach out for those shadowy figures from another dimension, the needle-like buildings, the dreams I half remember, faraway places I yearn for and could never reach. Until now. I call for them, pulling, clawing them toward me inch by inch.

*Let me go.*

Orpheus's fingers tighten against my jaw.

And then –

The corridor in front of me glitches. Staticky bits of wall go black and flicker out of existence. At the very edges of my vision, I see jagged edges, shimmering against the plane of reality.

And then it all falls away: the walls, the floor, the too-bright lights. Even the muffled howl of wind and rain disappears. Everything goes silent. And all around me grows that crushing press, that horrible fall into darkness, that inevitability.

*Yes.*

I feel a growing, palpable certainty. I'm on my way. If I can just go a little farther, if I can just keep going . . .

My ears pop.

And then the pressure relents, just as quickly as it came.

I fall to my knees, and the world before me is new: Rolling hills of indigo lead to alien forests rising up beyond. A purple blanket of trees drapes over distant foothills. Jagged, unearthly mountains thrust miles upward to touch a black, star-swept sky. And there, up in the velvety sky, four alien moons glow down on me like a welcome.

I inhale deeply. Thick, sweet air fills my lungs. I've never smelled anything so clean, so fresh. I can smell the wet earth, the blooming flowers, the night breeze. This is new. This isn't the barren, dying Earth; this isn't anywhere in my solar system. This is alive, this is alien, and it feels holy. This is a new world. And I brought myself here. I opened a fucking door, and I walked through it.

Goosebumps rise on my skin. Holy shit.

Tension and fear leave my body as I dig my fingers into the indigo grass, raking my nails through dark, damp soil. I want to bury my face in this fresh flora. I never want to stop breathing this air. Imagine what I could experience here, the beauty. Unlike Earth, life persists here. This isn't a dying world. It's flourishing. A tear rolls down my cheek as I close my eyes and lean down, pressing a cheek to the grass.

I stay there for a long time, just breathing, reveling in the growing things around me. I could stay here forever. There's nothing stopping me.

But soon enough, distant thoughts come drifting in: Thoughts of my world, left behind. Orpheus, still in the vault. That thought alone cuts through the euphoria of this new world: *Orpheus*. If I leave him there, what will he do? He'll starve, or he'll leave. And if he leaves . . . Ian and Eros won't be the last of his victims.

Goddamn it. I have to go back. I can't leave him there.

'Fuck,' I murmur.

Before I change my mind, I close my eyes and exhale. I try to recreate what I did back in the vault. I recall the way it felt to open the door, the buzz against my skin, the glitch, the fall – and then it's happening, and I *am* falling, falling until the darkness swallows me. Only a few breaths later, and my knees slam to the concrete floor in Ian's vault.

'Welcome back,' Orpheus says.

I get to my feet, turning to face him. Adrenaline bursts through me again, my heart pounding, my breaths coming in gasps. I stare at Orpheus, and I know I should be afraid. I should be angry. But all I can think is –

'I did it,' I breathe. I crossed a bridge to another world. Twice. For a second, I don't even care that I'm back here in my own world, that nothing has changed.

Because I'm not just Katherine Fox, broke fringe science blogger. I'm Katherine Fox, the girl who can open fucking doors between universes. The realization blazes through me like a shot of the strongest liquor, every organ and cell in my body awash with the revelation. And when all the things that seemed impossible to me – all the jobs and dreams and loves I'd convinced myself I'd probably never have – come rushing back, I gloriously realize I don't care. I don't want them anymore. I want *more* than just jobs and loves. I want *the world*.

'Kit?' Orpheus says, but he makes no move to grab me again. He only stands there, watching, wary.

'Orpheus.' The air around me seems to vibrate, to crackle with energy. For the first time in my life, I feel untouchable.

Orpheus draws a hand down his face, and it's a painfully human gesture. 'I never wanted to come here,' he says, words falling out like a dam is breaking. 'Ian pulled me through and trapped me in this body. And when he realized what I was, what I needed, he tried to send me back. But the door would not open again. I only did what I had to, to survive.'

I listen, making no move to run, no move to silence him. And I realize, now, that I understand him – this otherworldly entity, this mind in the body of a beautiful machine. Ian was no genius. He was a floundering idiot with more money and ambition than smarts. A man who found a way to open a door, only to kidnap and imprison what he found on the other side.

And I see clearly that Orpheus is a victim, a prisoner here. A feral creature kept in a too-small cage until it's driven mad with hunger and rage. Even Eros knew that it was only a matter of time before Orpheus escaped. And that when he did, he would be ravenous.

But Eros and Ian didn't have a way out. They didn't have what I have. They were lesser; they were food. I thought I was in danger from Orpheus, but now . . . now, he doesn't frighten me at all. He'll never hurt me. I'm too powerful, too important. And I see the truth in his eyes.

'You're far from home,' I say, holding Orpheus's gaze. 'And you're hungry.'

'Yes.'

'But you won't eat me.'

'No.'

'Tell me why not.' I want to hear him say it.

There's a moment of silence while the wind shrieks outside, muffled and far away.

'Because you have ruined me,' Orpheus says. 'I'm broken beyond repair. In this infinite span of worlds, all I see is you. This body, this soul, all belong to you. If you asked me to, I'd die for you.'

I smile slowly. I relish the confession. Eat it up. It lights me up from the inside like a bolt of lightning, filling me with self-assured heat. Of course he worships me. Of course he would die for me. I can move between worlds. I'm fucking utterly rare. More powerful than anyone else on Earth.

And in his words I also hear the unspoken truth, the part he won't say out loud: *I need you.*

I never needed Ian De Leon's pathetic book.

A slow smile curves Orpheus's mouth. Like he can see what I'm thinking, and he approves.

'Orpheus,' I say, moving toward him. 'I –'

Before I can say anything more, he sweeps me into a kiss. It's fierce, desperate, our teeth and lips colliding. I wrap my arms around his neck and fall easily into him. There's no denying the connection between us, the comfort, the feeling of intimacy and reunion. He's a missing puzzle piece that fell into place the moment I first saw him down here in the vault. He showed me who I am. And in return, I'll let him worship me for as long as he wants.

I pull away from his kiss, gripping his shirt with my fists. 'Come with me.'

Because there's nothing left for us here. Not in this penthouse. Not in Los Angeles, not on Earth. And here, there can be no future with Orpheus. But in some other world . . .

'Where?' he asks. But I see it in his eyes. He'll go wherever I go. He'd follow me into Hell itself.

I lift my face to him. He's extraordinary, even here in the harsh light, even knowing that on either side of us are bodies, bodies *he* destroyed. His eyes glow honey-soft. He's the only one who's ever seen me as something more than a struggling writer, a bottle girl, a one-night stand.

I swallow a lump in my throat.

I'm going to forget this penthouse and everything that happened here.

So I reach out to the mirage, remembering the feeling it gave me, the pull, and with a flicker, it appears – a door in the wall, a jagged shape, swirling colors and shapes drawing my gaze inward.

'Somewhere else,' I say. 'Anywhere you want.'

Orpheus looks at the door, then back at me, his gaze full of wonder.

'We don't belong here.' I kiss his jaw, just below the ear. 'Come with me.'

He groans low in his throat, one hand tightening at the small of my back.

'Kit,' he murmurs. 'You perfect, beautiful . . .'

'Say yes,' I plead.

He kisses me, slow and sweet, holding me close like I'm the most precious thing in the world. He whispers my name into my neck over and over. Like he can't believe what I'm asking. Like he can't believe that I'm real.

The door shimmers in my periphery, kaleidoscopic, a question and a promise.

Breathless, grinning, with the door to another universe flickering next to me, I ask, 'Is that a yes?'

He pulls his mouth away, exhaling hot breath on my naked skin. Then his gaze lifts to mine. 'Kit Fox.' His golden eyes crackle with emotion. 'All you had to do was ask.'

'Then let's go.'

On a station platform, with nothing to read,
and a four-hour train journey stretching ahead of him...

That's where the story began for Penguin founder Allen Lane.
With only 'shabby reprints of shoddy novels' on offer,
he resolved to make better books for readers everywhere.

By the time his train pulled into London, the idea was formed.
He would bring the best writing, in stylish and affordable
formats, to everyone. His books would be sold in bookstores,
stationers and tobacconists, for no more than the price
of a ten-pack of cigarettes.

And on every book would be a Penguin, a bird with a certain
'dignified flippancy', and a friendly invitation to anyone who
wished to spend their time reading.

In 1935, the first ten Penguin paperbacks were published.
Just a year later, three million Penguins had made their
way onto our shelves.

Reading was changed forever.

—

A lot has changed since 1935, including Penguin, but in the
most important ways we're still the same. We still believe that
books and reading are for everyone. And we still believe that
whether you're seeking an afternoon's escape, a vigorous debate
or a soothing bedtime story, all possibilities open with a book.

Whoever you are, whatever you're looking for,
you can find it with Penguin.